THE QADI

AND THE

FORTUNE TELLER

THE QADI

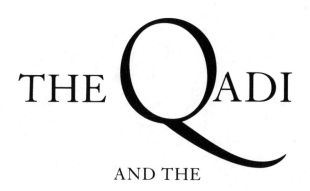

AND THE

FORTUNE TELLER

DIARY OF A JUDGE IN OTTOMAN BEIRUT
(1843)

NABIL SALEH

QUARTET BOOKS

First published by Quartet Books Limited in 1996
A member of the Namara Group
27 Goodge Street
London W1P 2LD

ISBN 0 7043 8019 6

A catalogue record for this book is available from the British Library.

Phototypeset in Great Britian by Contour Typesetters, Southall, London
Printed and bound in Great Britain by Staples Printers, Rochester Ltd.

To my wife and daughters

CONTENTS

ACKNOWLEDGEMENTS

Special thanks are due to **Ghazi Shaker** for his guidance and advice during the inception of this book; to **Omar Hamza** for his perceptive comments and knowledgeable suggestions; to **Antoine Kiwan** for providing me with historical books and for his wise counsel all along; to **Graham Handley** for his encouragement and for generously reading the manuscript and suggesting a number of modifications; to **Talal Farah** for giving me access to his personal library; to **Suad Mokbel Wensley** for finding the time to make the necessary research at the Public Record Office, Kew; to **Zelfa Hourani** for her valuable input; to **Nadim Shehadi** for sharing with me his vast knowledge of the period during which the story unfolds; to **Nawaf Salam** for the material he gave me; to **Jean Vanderpump** for her pertinent suggestions; and to **Kate Miles-Kingston** for her advice while she patiently typed several versions of my manuscript.

Two books by a Lebanese historian, **Hassan Hallaq**, were extremely useful, providing legal background for the year 1843 and inspiring some of the court cases described here. These books are *Awqaf al-muslimin fi Beirut* and *al-Tarikh al-ijtima'i wa al-iqtisadi wa al-siyasi*.

PREFACE

The diary kept by the Qadi (judge) of Beirut, Sheikh 'Abdallah bin Ahmad bin Abu Bakr al-Jabburi, known as Abu Khalid, which follows covers ten months of the year 1259 Hegira, which corresponds to 1843. This was a year of relative calm in Mount Lebanon and its coastal towns, an uneasy peace in the midst of years of turmoil occasioned by great and grave events.

These started when the Ottoman Sultan Mahmud II refused to give his nominal vassal Muhammad 'Ali of Egypt the complete reward he expected for the assistance he had provided to the Empire against the Greeks. Muhammad 'Ali decided to take Syria and Lebanon by force. In 1832 Ibrahim Pasha, Muhammad 'Ali's son, conquered and occupied that coveted part of the Ottoman Empire. Eygptian rule was not to last long, despite French backing and the full cooperation given by the Emir of Lebanon, Bashir Shehab II, the Great. Maronites and Druzes, encouraged by the Ottomans and the British, rebelled against the Egyptian Pasha.

On 11 September 1840 a joint British and Austrian fleet, under the command of Commodore Sir Charles Napier, bombarded Beirut, destroying large sections of the ancient walls and forts which protected the town. Meanwhile, Turkish, British and Austrian troops landed at the Bay of Junieh, north of Beirut, and joined the Lebanese fighters. In October 1840 the Egyptian forces collapsed and retreated towards Egypt. In their wake Emir Bashir went into exile in Malta, courtesy of the British Government.

Bashir III, from the same feudal Shehab family, was appointed Emir of Mount Lebanon, but he was incompetent and had been deposed by the end of 1842. During his short reign, bloody clashes occurred between Maronites and Druzes. Under Ibrahim Pasha, the former had enjoyed preferential treatment which allowed them to prosper, while the latter and their feudal chiefs were oppressed. As a result, most of their youth fled from military service, and when they returned from exile they were destitute. As Prosper Bourée, the French Consul in Beirut, observed in 1841, 'There is scarcely any piece of property about which a Christian and a Druze cannot have a case.' A trivial event between two villagers, one Christian and the other Druze, led to all-out war in the mountains and the Bekaa valley.

The European powers of the time – namely Britain, France, Russia, Austria and Prussia – pressed the Ottomans to intervene and put an end to the bloodshed. The Ottomans saw this as an opportunity to extend their direct rule over Mount Lebanon, in the same way that they controlled Beirut and all the coastal towns. They grasped the occasion and appointed one of their high-ranking officers as Governor of Mount Lebanon.

This did not please the consuls of the European powers and soon the Druzes revolted, but their resistance was put down by the Ottomans. Nevertheless, the latter had to give in to European pressure, and on 1 January 1843 Mount Lebanon was divided into two districts (*kaymacamiyyat*), one Christian and the other Druze. A Christian emir was appointed as *kaymacam* (head) of the former and a Druze emir *kaymacam* of the latter.

Disorder in Mount Lebanon was the pretext for, if not the consequence of, foreign intervention in the ailing Ottoman Empire's affairs. Beirut, a small town of roughly fifty acres within its walls and 15,000 inhabitants, including those who populated the immediate outskirts, was the seat of the powerful European consuls. To protect the numerous religious communities found on Lebanese soil was the alleged aim of foreign intervention, with much talk of the upholding of moral and humanitarian values. In reality, power politics provided a more potent motivation.

By 1843 Beirut had expanded beyond its walls, a process begun even before Ibrahim Pasha had removed parts of the ramparts and the British and Austrian fleet had destroyed most of what remained. The tragic events in Mount Lebanon had driven hundreds of destitute refugees into the town, which was fully controlled by the Ottomans and therefore peaceful. In addition the port of Beirut was vital for European business, and was consequently immune from contrived troubles. It attracted scores of new businessmen and intermediaries.

It is amidst this relatively calm but increasingly busy environment, not far removed from a tumultuous background, that Qadi Abu Khalid dipped his pen into a copper inkstand and confided his inner thoughts to his diary.

The diary reveals a great deal about the Qadi's personality, his family, his work and his problems, but not enough about his background, his milieu or even his features. The missing information was gleaned from contemporary papers which escaped the destruction of time.

Ahmad, Abu Khalid's father, was a craftsman who made copper kitchen utensils. He was poor and uneducated, but renowned for his honesty. He was also rather headstrong, and his wife Zeinab, Abu Khalid's mother, suffered all her life from that idiosyncrasy. They had married in 1799, the year Bonaparte besieged but could not take Acre.

Zeinab was raised in Sayda (ancient Sidon), some fifty miles from Acre, and her parents found in her marriage to a Beiruti a convenient way to move her further away from the danger of a foreign invasion. With the help of an intermediary known to both families, Zeinab left her birthplace and joined her husband in Beirut.

At exactly the turn of the nineteenth century 'Abdallah –

later to be known as Abu Khalid, from the name of his eldest son – was born to Ahmad and Zeinab.

Two other sons and three daughters followed, but the boys died in infancy. 'Abdallah's father and mother placed all their hopes on their only surviving son. Despite the family's hand-to-mouth existence, the little boy was well groomed and his parents made great sacrifices to enable him to attend the lessons of the blind sheikh of a nearby *zawiya* (a prayer room and a school). Years later 'Abdallah's master honoured him with a licence to teach Islamic jurisprudence and to issue opinions.

By that time 'Abdallah was a young man of twenty, rather short in height but with pleasant features. It was time for him to marry and start a family. His mother arranged the matchmaking. Young, educated bachelors being scarce, it was easy for her to choose as 'Abdallah's bride-to-be a girl whose mother had died at the time of her birth leaving her what seemed to the al-Jabburis a small fortune. The girl was not particularly good-looking, but she was not ugly either. Also, having known no mother, she became fond of her mother-in-law and did not find it abnormal that her husband's devotion and respect should be bestowed on his mother instead of her.

The marriage was eventually blessed by the birth of a son, Khalid, who came after two daughters, 'Aisha and Khadijah. 'Abdallah took immense pride in being referred to as Abu Khalid. As for Umm Khalid, she felt reassured that her marriage was consolidated by Khalid's arrival.

Soon Abu Khalid's reputation as an able jurist was to spread among his fellow citizens. In the year 1835 the office of Qadi became vacant in Beirut and he was the natural choice to fill it. His ascent could not be witnessed by his father, who had died a few years before, but his mother shed abundant tears of pride and joy.

Abu Khalid led a very well-regulated life. Three times a week he was on the bench, settling litigants' disputes and looking at various applications. Every Friday he went to the public bath to relax and listen to all sorts of gossip, without showing any apparent interest, and then he went to the mosque for communal prayers. Before sunset he was invariably at home for a solitary dinner prepared by his wife and his two daughters. Occasionally he invited his son to share his meal.

Abu Khalid's daily routine was not particularly stimulating to the mind: why, then, he felt the need to keep a journal – at a time when people hardly wrote, or even read – and why he did not pursue his endeavour longer than a few months will be, to some extent, explained by the Qadi himself.

The diary did not see the light of day until the late 1970s. It was hidden inside the wall of a house located in the centre of Beirut. The house was destroyed during an upsurge of fighting between Christians and Muslims. Once more the fighting was mostly instigated and fuelled by foreign powers, not exactly the same powers that had been active during the mid-nineteenth century but others who had replaced them, opportunistically playing the same roles and using the same pretexts. The only difference this time was that Beirut was not spared. On the contrary, it was a target; it was meant to be destroyed that other places might survive and prosper.

The leather-bound manuscript was taken by a freedom fighter to a foreign journalist, who bought it for a few dollars, attracted by its time-worn leather binding and its elegantly convoluted handwriting. Later on it caught the eye of the journalist's Lebanese mistress, who was constantly after what she called 'antiques', whether they were fake Roman figurines, Sèvres vases or second-hand books. From there, Abu Khalid's diary found its way to translation, annotation and, finally, publication.

THE QADI AND THE

AND THE

FORTUNE TELLER

Muharram 1259 H (January 1843)

*The Qadi's worries; greed takes the guise
of religious outrage; dragoman's visit to
the Qadi; the death of an innocent . . .*

In the Name of God, Most Gracious, Most Merciful

. . . I AM AWARE that committing ingenuous thoughts to paper is
careless at a time when one has to hide permanently behind a
façade and when what one says is more important than what
one thinks, so long as what one thinks is not made public. The
danger is greater nowadays, for our words and deeds are
listened to and watched by the omniscient agents of the
Governor As'ad Pasha.

Nevertheless, I feel an irresistible compulsion to confide in
someone; but whom? A diary, after all, will be much safer than
any friend who might one day turn against me or take
advantage of my confidence. This diary will have to be well
hidden; that will be my responsibility and I know I can assume
it. What I cannot be sure of is how long a friend will remain as
such, and how long a confidant will keep a secret to himself.

Since I made the promise to be honest, at least with myself, I
must add that this diary will also be my justification and
vindication, sparing me incredulous or ironic looks, malignant
remarks or vicious retaliation.

I have been told that I am under suspicion by the authorities
for having collaborated with the Egyptians. Allah be my
witness, whatever I did during Ibrahim Pasha's rule was to
survive, which is always at a price. Others, and I know them
individually, have enriched themselves by speculating, hoard-
ing food and selling their souls. They hold high offices and the

9

new administration shows them every sign of respect. I never did anything that they did, having had neither the opportunity nor the choice, but still I have been told in confidence by Abu Kasim (the Qadi's best friend) that the Governor does not like me. I am not so sure that Abu Kasim is telling the truth. He has the Governor's ear, but he is so scheming, so manipulative, that he might have made up the whole story to drive me out of the way so that Abu Mazen, his cousin, could be appointed Qadi – as if the position is worth fighting over. True, I am held in some esteem by the community, but I receive no fixed salary, despite the promise that all civil servants were given by the authorities as early as 1256 H (1840). A fee is all I take from the litigant who wins his case, and the winner is seldom grateful once his position is established. Only fear could loosen his purse, but fear is immediately wiped out by a favourable ruling and replaced instead by resentment because it took so long to vindicate him.

Moreover, the number of cases to be administered by the Qadi has dwindled considerably. Commercial suits are tried by the provincial *majlis* (council); since 1256 criminal cases have been part of the jurisdiction of the *mutasallem* (civil governor), while foreigners who belong to countries of some standing are subject to the complete jurisdiction of consular officers in civil and criminal cases. What is left to the Qadi is to deal with matters of personal status, property holdings and the like, as well as *awkaf* (charitable endowments).

With such restricted jurisdiction, it is nearly impossible for an honest Qadi to lead a decent life.

. . . I AM REALLY WORRIED about what Abu Kasim told me. My first reaction was to dismiss what he said, but on reflection he might be telling the truth and my fate could well be sealed by now. I will be either disgracefully dismissed from office or, worse, condemned to exile.

. . . I MET the *Mufti* (a person learned in the *sharia*) in the public *hammam* (bath) of Bab al-Serail. It was no coincidence. I knew that he went there regularly, every Friday, and I intended to test his reaction when he saw me. He was bound to know something. I entered the large room, which was lit by small cupolas with stained-glass sections. Sheikh Ahmed was resting on a pile of cushions laid down on the multicoloured marble floor. He had just finished being bathed by the black slaves in attendance.

He signalled to me to sit next to him and showed me all the signs of kindness and consideration. I was totally relieved and reassured about my future, yet the future is in the hands of Allah alone.

> *Truly it is He, the Beneficent, the Merciful.*
> Qur'an, s. LII, 28

... MY MIND AT PEACE, I am now ready to resume my charge. I will need all my moral strength to adjudicate a disturbing case brought to my court.

Wardeh is the young and beautiful widow of the *dhimmi* Butros 'Azar, who died, leaving to their only son, Tanios, aged five, large real estate properties in the Mountains. What he did not do was to designate a guardian for him. My predecessor appointed Wardeh to be such a guardian.

During the bloody events which made the Mountains grieve, Wardeh's village was destroyed and most of the villagers killed. Wardeh and Tanios owed their lives to the compassion of a young Druze warrior, who helped them escape to Beirut.

The two settled in the town in great poverty, but when peace was restored Wardeh, owing to her intelligence and ability, was able to reclaim all her son's inheritance. Fate brought her's and her son's saviour together. They immediately fell in love and decided to marry. They could achieve that only by both converting to Islam, because their respective religious authorities would not celebrate a mixed marriage. Hence they joined the ranks of the true believers.

For the young Druze warrior, his conversion to Islam brought no major difficulties. Not only was he poor and no one really cared about his religious state of mind, but most importantly his religion of birth permitted him to pretend to adopt any other religion, whenever necessary or simply convenient. For his fellow men, he would remain a Druze whether he uttered the *shehada* (the statement of belief in the dogma of Islam) or received baptism.

Not so for Wardeh. Her conversion caused an enormous scandal, fuelled by the family of her late husband. The family saw Tanios's wealth passing under the effective, if not legal, control of a hated and feared enemy. That was unacceptable. Greed took the guise of religious outrage.

A delegation from the family went to Bkerkeh to see the Maronite Patriarch, who prudently advised them to settle the matter amicably. The Patriarch's advice was heeded and as a compromise Wardeh agreed to resign her duties as Tanios's guardian, provided her brother was appointed instead.

That is why they came to me. I am not convinced that Wardeh should be relieved of her duties under the alleged pretence that she does not really care about Tanios. I know for a fact that she cares. I know her personally. During the period of her predicament and destitution, she used to come to our house as a cleaning lady, bringing Tanios with her. I can bear witness to the way she treated him, and I have followed her endeavour and eventual success in reclaiming his inheritance.

Unfortunately, the teaching of our Master Abu Hanifa does not allow me to rely upon personal knowledge unless it is acquired during the exercise of my duties.

I need more time to reflect before giving any ruling.

> *Come not nigh to the orphan's property except to improve it.*
>
> Qur'an, s. XVII, 34

. . . CLOSE TO HOME and the Great Mosque of 'Umar is the

courthouse. When I went early in the morning, the small front garden was already full of litigants and witnesses. I entered the room and sat cross-legged on the low sofa opposite the door. My clerk sat on the ground on a mat of rushes, as did the *shuhud al-hal* (the witnesses of the proceedings).

I read a petition signed by Wardeh requesting to be relieved of her duties as guardian of her son, Tanios. The letter was handed over by Wardeh's brother, who expressed his willingness to be such a guardian.

I listened to four witnesses brought by the brother, each of whom testified to his suitability for such a responsibility. Having given the case ample consideration, I reached the conclusion that it was not up to me to investigate the real motives behind the apparent ones – *O ye who believe, avoid suspicion (as much as possible), for suspicion in some cases is a sin* (Qur'an, s. XLIX, 12) – or to rely on a personal knowledge acquired long before the case was brought to my court. Most of all, I did not want to get involved in any wrangling between the Christian and Druze religious authorities or, worse, render Tanios the victim of such quarrels. Therefore I granted the petition.

. . . AFTER THE EVENING prayer I was about to eat the dinner prepared and served by Umm Khalid and my two daughters, 'Aisha and Khadijah. The dinner consisted of courgettes stuffed with minced meat and rice, accompanied by a bowl of *laban* (yoghurt) and bread. Close to me on the mattress sat Khalid, my son, the light of my eyes and the joy of my heart. Khalid is only ten years old and is very promising. I teach him the Qur'an, which he has to know by heart. When that is achieved, he will be rewarded by a big celebration which will make the neighbours and guests die with envy while publicly partaking in our joy.

Loud bangs on the front door woke me from these inviting prospects. No unannounced visitor would ever come to me or to any decent house after sunset. It cannot but be bad news.

Could it be a summons to see the Pasha, who is so prompt to lend a favourable ear to the least credible delation?

My young servant – not yet eleven, so the women of the house do not have to cover their faces in his presence – brought a letter. On his knees he handed it over to me, while shouting that the messenger was waiting outside for my answer. Despite all efforts, I have failed to make him lower his voice; he regards shouting an important part of his function.

I broke the red seal and unfolded the letter. It was from one of the dragomans of the British Consulate. The dragoman, whom I have met on one or two occasions, requested an appointment on an urgent matter.

I was greatly puzzled and my curiosity aroused. I made an appointment for him on the following day in the afternoon, not willing to wait any longer to satisfy my curiosity and the request of such an important personage.

. . . THE DRAGOMAN, Mr Saba, entered the visitors' room. He was handsome and wore an impressive uniform adorned with golden braid. A sword flapped at his tightly trousered left leg whenever he made a move. He greeted me with all marks of respect, without losing any of his nobility. His entire demeanour indicated a powerful person with the dignity conferred by a mighty sponsor, in this instance the British Empire.

We both reclined on piles of cushions and the boy brought coffee and two long pipes. We exchanged all sorts of compliments for a time, then, when I ordered two new pipes and more coffee, Mr Saba clapped his hands. His servant, who was waiting in the corridor, was obviously expecting such a sign, for he entered the room where we were and put a big parcel in front of me.

'Some Kurani tobacco, which I beg you to accept as a token of friendship,' said Mr Saba. I thanked him aloud while privately marvelling at his knowledge of my taste for that brand of tobacco, which I appreciate for its perfume and because it is much milder than the Jbeili brand.

More time passed, then my visitor stood up to leave. This is the moment when the real motive behind any visit is revealed, otherwise rules of good manners would be broken.

'Sheikh 'Abdallah,' said my visitor, 'I need your advice on a matter which will necessarily come to your knowledge in a day or two, unless you are already aware of it.' He paused for a short while and then carried on: 'A terrible and sad misfortune has occurred. The young son of Mustafa Fakhri was killed accidentally by the young servant of Mr Nash, the British merchant whom you know, or have heard of. The two youths, two good friends, were playing with a loaded gun, and while so doing the gun was fired and Mustafa's son was instantly killed. Mr Nash's servant is in hiding and the victim's father – whom Mr Nash has met to try to negotiate a settlement – declines to listen to any reason and demands the *kassas* (death penalty) for the perpetrator of this unfortunate incident, which he refuses to see as an accident.'

At this point Mr Saba added with emphasis, 'Sheikh 'Abdallah, we cannot allow the poor boy to be put to death; he did not intend to kill. If he were to be executed, that would be unacceptable and most of all would badly reflect on us. People would start thinking that our protection is worthless.'

From the seriousness of his voice, I understood that it was not only Mr Saba who wanted my help but also his great Queen. I took my time in deep reflection, just to make my visitor aware of the effort I needed to satisfy them.

After a fairly long silence, I uttered the following advice: 'I know Mustafa Fakhri; he is a good man but very stubborn. Money means less to him than public acclaim for his steadfast refusal to accept the *diyya* (blood money). There is also the fact that he does not want to be seen as selling his grief; that grief is genuine, for the victim is the son on whom he had placed all his hopes.

'Indeed, Mustafa has another son who is of age, but the one left is a good-for-nothing. All his time is spent in Beirut's numerous cafés, playing backgammon and drinking God knows what. Nevertheless, this remaining son is among the victim's heirs and as such is entitled to a share of the *diyya* and, most importantly, to waive the *kassas* that otherwise would befall the author of the homicide. When such a waiver is made even by just one of the heirs, no *kassas* could ever apply because a death penalty is not divisible.'

> *But if anyone remits the retaliation by way of*
> *charity, it is an act of atonement for himself.*
>   Qur'an, s. V, 48

'A final word of advice, Mr Saba. Do not yourself meet the son but send one of your stable-lads to him. That will cost you much less. Your deal is guaranteed anyway.'

. . . THIS IS THE DAY of the week for Umm Khalid, 'Aisha and Khadijah to visit the cemetery and pay their respects to the dead of our families.

Their visit to the cemetery, just outside Bab al-Serail, has become a weekly routine, a saintly occasion for them to get out of the house. What is also customary is for Umm Khalid to request my permission for venturing outside and for me to grant it. Nevertheless, I make it a point that permission has to be solicited each time, otherwise God knows what disorders might happen.

What made this day special was that Khalid, my son, started taking private lessons in syntax and grammar. His teacher is *muallem* (master) Shibli Bu Khatir, a *dhimmi* who teaches a new method devised by a Maronite Bishop of Aleppo. With this method, rules of grammar and syntax can be mastered within two years' instead of the usual ten years. I also hope that in the process Khalid will learn rudiments of the Italian language, acquired by *muallem* Shibli during his early years abroad.

I made my acquaintance with *muallem* Shibli when he appeared before me as the witness of a sale transaction involving a farm located on the outskirts. In the process of examining him and also during the procedure of *tazkiya* (attesting the reliability of a witness through other witnesses), I came to like him and to appreciate his vast knowledge of grammar and literature. He told me about the Bishop's new method and I decided to entrust Khalid to his scholarly care. One has to go along with progress.

Hence Umm Khalid, accompanied by Khalid and his sisters, instead of going straight to the cemetery, passed into Souk al-Cotton (the cotton market) and left Khalid in the Christians' quarter, where *muallem* Bu Khatir lives.

When they all returned home, I asked Khalid whether Bu Khatir had made any religious intimation during the lesson. I was pretty sure that the answer would be no, as it indeed was. I wanted, however, to be fully satisfied that *muallem* Shibli was not one of those missionaries who are nowadays swarming all over the place in search of naïve or calculating converts.

Reassured, I turned to Umm Khalid, who was waiting on the side, very proud of her son. She guessed my next question and said, 'Yes, I have repositioned the flowers laid by 'Aisha and Khadijah on your mother's grave.'

That had nothing to do with any superstition. Actually Abu Kassim, who has grown-up sons, has informed me that young men and girls communicate with each other through the way bunches of flowers and palm-tree leaves are arranged on graves – perhaps a macabre but nevertheless inventive way to send signals of love. I wish I had known it during my youth. I will teach it to Khalid when he comes of age.

O God, help me to protect 'Aisha and Khadijah from evil.

. . . AN UNFAMILIAR agitation in the street woke me up. It was not the water-carrier's day and anyhow, despite all his usual thoughtlessness, he does not normally generate such a tumult.

I clapped my hands but no one came to attend to my needs and satisfy my curiosity. After performing my ablutions and morning prayer, I went in search of someone who would tell me what was going on. Eventually I found Umm Khalid in the outdoor kitchen, weeping silently. She had Khalid pressed against her heart, while with a spoon in her right hand she stirred one of her recipes in the biggest cauldron of the house.

'What is the matter, woman? Why are you in that state?' I asked. In a frail voice the reply came: 'These are ill-fated days for Abu 'Abbas and his family, our neighbours. They took refuge in Beirut from the Mountains' bloody clashes but misfortune knows no boundaries. You probably recall that I sought your advice about the custody of young Zein, the son of Abu 'Abbas's youngest daughter; he got along so well with our Khalid, despite being much younger. The mother was married to a fellow Druze, not from Lebanon's Mountains but from Djebel Hauran. After a couple of years she came back to her father's house with Zein in her custody. You certainly recall that some months ago Zein disappeared, leaving his mother and the whole family in total anguish, not knowing whether he was alive or dead until the news reached us here that he had been snatched by his father and taken to Djebel Hauran.

'The most distressing thing happened a few days ago. Zein's mother dreamed that her son was running towards her, his hands stretched out, calling for her help. Umm 'Abbas and I tried to calm her down, telling her that she had had a nightmare and nothing else, but neither of us could bring her to reason, so convinced was she that Zein was in mortal danger.'

Umm Khalid paused, wiping away her tears, then proceeded: 'Early this morning a messenger brought the news to Abu 'Abbas that his grandson had died. The carrier of that terrible announcement gave the following account: Zein was playing in the courtyard of his father's house, being looked after by his stepmother, the father having remarried a woman from his own tribe. The stepmother went inside the house for a couple of minutes – so she said – and when she came out, Zein could not be found anywhere. Eventually he was discovered dead at the bottom of the cistern which stands in the middle of the courtyard.

'As soon as the news spread through the neighbourhood, friends and acquaintances flocked to grieve with Abu 'Abbas and his family. I am preparing some food for the mourners and all the neighbours are doing the same. Umm 'Abbas is not in her right mind to think about these matters. You do not mind my initiative, I hope?'

I dismissed these last words offhandedly; it was not a time for minor details. I have known Abu 'Abbas since he took refuge in peaceful Beirut, escaping from the armed conflicts which locked Christians and Druzes in opposition, and continue to split them since the Emir's exile. Despite his being a member of a heretical sect, I came to appreciate and respect Abu 'Abbas as a charitable man who kept his word at whatever cost. I felt very sorry for him, for Umm 'Abbas and especially for Zein's mother.

> *Those whose lives the angels take in a state*
> *of purity' saying to them: Peace be on you,*
> *enter ye the Garden, because of the good ye did.*
> Qur'an, s. XVI, 32.

Comes the night I am sure that Khalid will sleep against his mother's heart. I myself shall pray Allah to protect us from wrongdoers.

. . . I CANNOT remove from my mind Zein's image and the memory of the terribly sad fate which uprooted this young flower from the bosom of his loving family. O Allah; spare me any such ordeal. Protect Khalid from evil. If anything were to happen to him, I should certainly not last long. When my beloved son was born after two daughters, nobody believed he would live; he was small and very weak. The midwife who delivered him hastened to leave lest his soul depart the little body while she was still at hand. She was not prepared to bear any responsiblity for what she considered to be a hopeless case. But Khalid was to live, by Allah's favour. Had he died, it would also have been His will, and I would have accepted His decree with sadness but submission. After all, who am I to question His verdicts?

Khalid, for my joy, lived. Indeed, he was and still is much smaller and much weaker than other children of the same age, but at least he is here to brighten my days and support me when I reach old age. Because of Khalid's frailty, I have had to intervene more than once to protect him from bullies who take advantage of his tender age and good heart.

Only yesterday he came home crying his eyes out. That upset and worried me. He readily confided in me, accusing Sa'eb, a playmate, of having beaten him for no reason except that he had honestly reported to Sa'eb's mother a prank that her devil of a son had devised to frighten an old lady. Sa'eb had covered himself in a white sheet and made terrifying sounds in the room of the poor lady, who believed she was being visited by a ghost. She hurriedly went out, telling of the dreadful apparition and of her narrow escape from a non-return trip to the abyss. Sa'eb's father gave him a memorable thrashing.

Not long after, Sa'eb took revenge on Khalid and promised more. Only harsh words to the boy's parents put an end to the persecution of my innocent son. I do not understand why 'Aisha and Khadijah are angry with Khalid, who, after all, was driven by good intentions. This boy of ten will show the world his worth when his time comes. I will give him education and means to perpetuate my name with honour. With God's help, he will not fail me.

. . . I HAVE TO SUPPLEMENT the meagre income I get from my profession. Thus I occasionally engage in trade, not in an active way but as an investor in a *mudaraba* (commenda or limited partnership). What I do is provide an amount of money to a *mudarib* (agent-manager), who is to trade with it in an agreed manner. The agent-manager buys goods, sells them for the best price possible and divides the profits between us after deducting his expenses.

The three requisites for a successful *mudaraba* are the honesty and ability of the agent-manager and, most of all, God's blessing. If it were otherwise, the investor would lose his money as surely as night follows day.

The Prophet – peace be on him – used to repeat, 'Allah says, I am third with two partners unless one betrays the other.' He himself was the best of agent-managers for the wealthy widow Khadijah, whom he later married.

My agent-manager, Gerios Antoun, has all the right attributes, except that he is not a true believer. I am, however, confident that such an educated and upright man will one day be led to the true religion. My dealings with him may even hasten the process.

At the age of six, he was sent by his father to a missionary school recently started in Beirut by the Protestant Church. Promptly he acquired knowledge of the English language. It was not enough for him, so within a few years he arranged to be taught French and Italian by some foreign priests. With the wealth of four languages, he threw himself into business, dealing more particularly with foreign visitors and residents. In no time he accumulated a vast fortune but, very wisely, he continues to lead a quiet and low-profile life.

One day, after he had completed a very successful transaction, I joked with him: 'Two transactions such as this one, O Gerios, and you will be able to move to a bigger house, acquire a new horse and still have enough money left to envisage matrimony.'

Gerios smiled and replied, 'You know me better, O Abu Khalid. Rest assured, I will never overstep my position and attract too much attention to myself and my trade. When I was young and burning with ambition, my father used to repeat for my benefit the following story. The Caliph Haroun al-Rashid asked Abu Nawwas, "Who is enjoying life most?" The reply came, "He who has a house to receive him, a wife to take care of him – and whom we do not know."

'Abu Khalid, I will marry one day, but I will never do

anything which might "open the eye" (attract attention) on me.'

Lately I gave this good man a number of *darahem* (sing. *dirham*; one of the many Ottoman currencies then in circulation) for him to trade for our joint benefit. It was agreed that he would go to Damascus and buy cashmere shawls, velvets and other materials which could be sold in Beirut at a higher price, leaving us with a handsome profit to share.

Soon after Gerios's departure for Damascus, all roads between that city and Beirut were cut off by heavy snow, which covered the whole of the Mountains. I was not expecting to see him for a month at least. To my utmost surprise he was, this very afternoon, clapping his hands at the door of my house to give the *hareem* time to disappear from sight. This is the story he told me.

'While I was in Damascus, the Pasha decreed the devaluation of the *dirham* by ten per cent. It meant that with the money in my hand I would not be able to buy all the goods I intended to acquire for our venture.

'I knew that the news of the Pasha's decree could not reach Beirut for at least a fortnight, even by using the north road, so I decided to leave immediately, come back here and change our coins before the decree of devaluation reaches the town.

'I asked the muleteer Saïd, who was stranded in Damascus on account of the weather, if, despite the appalling road conditions, we could start for Beirut immediately. He replied that not for at least a month should one even contemplate passing across the Mountains on horseback.

'I enquired, "What about making the journey on foot?"

'"Only the lad Rafful can do it. He can walk on snow like a bird and he knows all the passes."

'I struck a deal with Rafful, who agreed to be my guide for a fee of seventy piastres.

'I put some of the coins in a belt round my waist and the rest inside a stick. I had even bought more coins at the devaluated rate, and a few other items. The latter I carried ostentatiously, to use as a decoy in case we were attacked by bandits. After a prayer to the Almighty, we started our journey, which took four hellish days.

'I did not stop at home; instead I came straight here to tell you that all is well. The money is safe. First thing tomorrow, I will start changing the coins. I will do that gradually, in order not to attract too much attention and raise suspicion.'

I strongly recommend to Gerios that all money-changing operations he intends to do be transacted hand-to-hand, because delaying completion of the exchange would be *riba* (usury). He promised to comply scrupulously with my directives.

SAFAR 1259 (February 1843)

The Qadi *reminisces; a second visit*
from the dragoman; the first Christian faqih; *a stroll*
outside the city's walls; bad neighbours; an
argument between an Austrian Jew and a Muslim . . .

. . . MY OLDEST friend is 'Abdel Ghaffar Halabi, known today as Abu Kasim, Kasim being the name of his first male offspring. Together we grew up and learned the Qur'an, the Hadith (the record of actions and sayings of the Prophet), grammar and arithmetic.

We attended those lessons at the *zawiya* located next to Jami' al-Nawfara (the Mosque of the Fountain). Our master was a blind sheikh, most redoubtable, for he was somehow able to perceive all that was going on round him. With his dreaded long and flexible reed he could reach any target from where he sat, guided solely by the murmuring of a voice or the breathing of a culprit. Over the five years during which I attended the master's lessons, I did not give him one occasion to throw his cane in my direction.

Maybe I was not the brightest pupil, but I was certainly the most attentive one. The reciting of the Qur'an captured my heart – although its meaning was revealed to me much later – and the Hadith caught my imagination. I longed to follow the path trodden by the Prophet and his Companions.

Arithmetic was not a matter I could master. Even now I have to proceed carefully whenever I have to apply to a specific case the rules of inheritance as revealed in the sacred Book.

Arithmetic was all that 'Abdel Ghaffar was interested in. No other subject mattered to him and whenever arithmetic was not taught, he was unable to concentrate his attention for more than a few seconds. This meant that any other lesson was punctuated by blows from the master's cane showered on his shoulders and head.

Not surprisingly I and 'Abdel Ghaffar took different directions when we attained adulthood. I went to Sheikh Yahya 'Afra and begged for some of his time so he could familiarize me with the *fiqh* (Islamic jurisprudence) according to the teaching of Abu Hanifa al-Na'man. I studied with Sheikh Yahya *Kitab al-Dur al-Mukhtar Sharh Tanwir al-Absar*, together with its commentaries by Sheikh Ahmad al-Tahtawi. After a while my master honoured me with a licence to teach and issue *fatawa* (responses).

'Abdel Ghaffar, as expected, went into business. He started as a coffee-boy, working for an elderly shop-owner in Souk al-Bazerkhan (market for fabrics, textiles and sewing materials). Eventually he married the shop-owner's only daughter, acquired his father-in-law's shop and established a prosperous workshop, where the most beautiful silk belts are woven.

Money brought to Abu Kasim the respect and prominence he always wanted. I must say that he accepts the marks of respect with such grace and elegance that those who give them are most grateful to him.

Quite naturally Abu Kasim was elected sheikh of the souk, and he was given the coveted honour of being the keeper of the keys of one of the city's gates. His duties consist of bearing the expenses of a lantern suspended at the gate and lit at sunset, and of remitting the keys of the gate in his charge to the Governor for safekeeping at night. That was, of course, before large sections of the ramparts were destroyed by the British naval bombardment.

Abu Kasim should be a contented man, but he is not. He is most unhappy with his wife, who cannot resist reminding him of his humble origins and recent riches, which were somehow acquired at her father's expense, at least at the beginning of Abu Kasim's successful rise to prominence. Indeed, she does not dare to voice her resentment and disdain or to fail in her duties, but she manages, one way or the other, to make those feelings known to her husband. Until now he does not wish to get rid of her – for he still gets satisfaction out of having married above his station. I wonder how much longer he is going to endure her scornful attitude, which sets a bad example for all other women.

. . . MR SABA, the British Consulate's dragoman, came to see me after prior notice of his visit. Our meeting was less formal than when we first met. He thanked me for my advice concerning the fatal accident to Mustafa Fakhri's son, a matter settled amicably by now, and we both sat comfortably cross-legged, surrounded by cushions, deriving satisfaction from a developing friendship as well as from our pipes.

This time Mr Saba wore Oriental dress and I noticed his dark-coloured turban as soon as he entered the room. I appreciated the mark of respect that he wished to convey to me by not wearing a white turban, which was a Muslim's prerogative until the time the Egyptian ruler made it available to the *dhimmis* as well. Mr Saba's gesture was especially noteworthy, for a man of his standing could have worn any colour he wanted, even before the Eygptian enfranchisement.

After the usual exchange of compliments, he brought up the subject of his visit in these terms: 'Abu Khalid, you are certainly aware that our work at the Consulate is not entirely devoted to important matters. We, from time to time, deal with insignificant problems. We have to; it is part of our duties towards our citizens and towards the people we protect. It is on a point of minor importance that I beg your indulgence, and appeal to your generosity and broad-mindedness.

'You may remember Basil, the magnificent *kavass* (an armed attendant) who used to accompany the Consul, Colonel Rose, wherever he went, walking the streets in front of him to move aside beggars and petitioners. That man, who seemed indestructible, has suddenly died in his sleep. His widow, a devout Christian, begged the Consul to muster all his influence so that the customary word *halaka* does not figure in the Burial Order that you will issue; instead either *tawafa* or *mata* should be used.

'In vain I tried to explain to her that all three words have the same meaning, "has died". She adamantly refused to listen to my explanations. For her, *halaka* meant that her husband's soul was damned, and I must admit that in Christian theological terminology it means just that.'

I remained silent for a few minutes, pondering upon the real motivation behind Mr Saba's request. Is it as innocent as it appears to be or does it hide something more sinister? Is it intended to obtain, through me, more concessions in favour of the *dhimmis* or is it only a plea prompted by real religious scruples?

I like Mr Saba and I would hate to turn down his request, which appears to be a small favour concerning a minor private matter. On the other hand, he is the agent of a powerful empire which extends its protection to all the *dhimmis*, who are in the first place the subjects of HM the Sultan. That seemingly innocent request could well be used as a precedent for more important concessions in favour of the *dhimmis*.

Not knowing what answer I should give Mr Saba, I finally said, '*Inshallah khair*' (God willing, good is to be expected).

With that ambivalent remark he departed.

. . . I HAVE SIGNED Basil's Burial Order and made it conform to the wording wanted by his widow. I reached my decision after a long night of reflection, always going back to the fundamental question which kept arising: who am I to turn away a request made by the representative of the second most powerful nation on earth, especially when what he asks for is nothing more than a linguistic substition in a miserable order given by the humble servant of the Sultan, the mightiest of all rulers on earth, who has bestowed his favour on the supplicant's master? Who am I to stand between the powerful and the mighty? God has mercy for the humble who denies vanity.

But God will cancel anything (vain) that Satan throws in . . .

Qur'an, s. XXII, 52

Slowly, painfully, I came to the decision I have reached, asking myself why I cannot have someone near who would lend a sympathetic ear to my anguish and provide me with wise advice in return. More than once I was tempted to share my problems with Umm Khalid; each time I listened to the voice of reason and abstained. Umm Khalid would lose all respect for me if she were to be made aware of my inner thoughts, my doubts and my fears.

. . . MR SABA'S SERVANT brought me a fine white *'aba* (an ample sleeveless coat, open at the front, worn on top of the usual garment) and a superb cashmere shawl. It was a silk *'aba* decorated with gold braid on the front and the back. It must have cost at least five hundred silver *asadi* piastres. As for the shawl, I could not assess its value offhand, although it must have cost a small fortune. I know Abu Mitri, the man from Baghdad who imports similar shawls from India. I will get from him all I need to know about prices.

With these two precious gifts came Mr Saba's most urbane note. It was written on blue paper and to my extreme surprise it was not folded and sealed but inserted into a wrapper made of the same blue paper. That inventive weather-proof way to secure confidentiality left me full of admiration. This is what Mr Saba wrote:

To the most respected and learned authority,
to the pride of the governors and governed,

I beg you to accept the modest gift carried by your slave. It is far from being worthy of your rank but represents a mere token of my deep esteem and profound veneration.

Your humble servant,
Faddul Saba Ibn Ne'meh
Dragoman of Her Majesty's Consulate

I showed the *'aba* and cashmere shawl to Umm Khalid. Her only reaction was to say, 'He could have sent something for the house.'

. . . SHEIKH BSHARA AL-KHURI is the most astonishing of men. He is a Christian from Rashmayya (a small village in the Lebanese Mountains), who, against the odds, acquired a licence to teach the Islamic *fiqh*. The idea of acquainting himself with the *fiqh* came to Bshara after Emir Bashir Shehab II, the Great, ordered judges sitting in the Christian part of Mount Lebanon to derive their judgments from the Islamic *sharia*. Bshara approached the Emir and the Maronite Patriarch for them to fund his studies of the *sharia*, and to help him find a suitable teacher. The first part of the enterprise was rather easy; finding a teacher proved more difficult. After the sudden death of his first teacher and when potential others turned him down for fear of losing their credibility and standing among the community if they were to teach a *dhimmi* matters pertaining to religion, Bshara eventually found a mentor in Sheikh A'rabi al-Zayla' of Tripoli. Having studied with Sheikh A'rabi for a full seven months, Sheikh Bshara was finally rewarded for his studious persistence and given licence to teach *fiqh* and provide opinions in law. He then came to me and requested permission to attend my court as an observer, in order to learn more about the practice of the law. I gladly gave him leave to do so.

The downfall of the Great Emir, following the collapse of the Egyptian regime, made many assume a distant position from the members of the Shehab family. Those with a certain sense of decency left were content to avoid their company; others made them responsible for all ills. Some with fewer scruples attempted to take advantage of the collapse of the feudal regime and filed extravagant lawsuits with the courts. It was on the occasion of entertaining one such case that I came to appreciate the strength of Sheikh Bshara's character, besides his vast knowledge and skill. His sense of obligation towards the Great Emir remained unaffected after the latter's misfortune. That is in itself amazing, for how many times have we not seen the beneficiary of a favour turning against his benefactor the moment the latter's strength wanes, in order to alleviate the weight of his debt, if not disowning it altogether? Bshara's mind is contemptuous of such pettiness; he rushed to the defence of the Emir Shebab as soon as his assistance was needed.

That Emir owns in the district of Jbeil (ancient Byblos) a vast orchard in which grow various citrus trees. Soon after the Shehabs' fall, a man by the name of Jebraeel Mussa occupied the orchard, alleging that the property belonged to his family although it had been in the Shehabs' hands for many years past. He said that only fear of the Shehabs prevented him and his father and grandfathers before him from claiming back the property, and that, now that fear was dispelled, it was only fair and just that he retake possession of the orchard.

It was Sheikh Bshara who introduced an instance against Jebraeel Mussa, on behalf of the Emir Shehab. After the existence of the parties' respective powers of attorney was established by the usual way of oral evidence, Mussa's attorney was required to name his witnesses in order to substantiate his client's allegation of ownership.

I accepted the testimony of only one of Mussa's two witnesses, for the other one was deemed unreliable. That was the moment chosen by Sheikh Bshara to raise an exception based on the fact that Jebraeel Mussa had admitted in front of two witnesses that the orchard belonged to the Emir. Sheikh Bshara named those witnesses, who were heard and confirmed Mussa's admission.

Mussa's attorney challenged one of them on the ground that he was a professional witness, prepared to make any false statement under oath, for a fee. I required from the attorney evidence in support of his accusation to be provided within a reasonable time. He and his client left the court for that purpose and the case was postponed until the time one of the litigants should come back to me with new facts or requests.

... IT WAS ONE of those days which made me feel the urge to escape from the tumult and gloominess of the city. The weather was unusually mild for this time of the year, so I decided to take a stroll outside the crumbling ramparts. I wore a heavy 'aba and went through the maze of narrow, noisy and above all dirty streets; beggars, pedlars and donkeys were everywhere. The few small places left bare were as usual taken over by stall-keepers, a number of them refugees from the Mountains, yelling the most seductive words meant to attract attention to their goods on display. The traditional street vendors need no such fuss; it is enough for them to shout the name of the goods carried on their backs in containers and intermittently to produce, with tiny bells or handle-less cups, tinkling sounds which make their presence known and indicate the nature of their goods. It is either coffee, sus (a macerated drink of liquorice and tamarind), 'ayran (yoghurt diluted with water and seasoned with thyme, a little crushed garlic or dried mint) or simply drinking water.

Habitually I do not mind street cacophony, sometimes I even enjoy it; or could it be that in reality I enjoy the respectful greetings that I attract whenever I leave home? Would such a place, with all its dirt, narrow-mindedness and lack of horizons still seem gratifying if I were not an eminent member of its community, deriving my pride from others' sub-servience?

I brushed aside these thoughts, which could be unhealthy, and I rushed towards Bab-Idriss (the west gate) in search of peace and open space. On my way it suddenly came to me that Abu Kasim's company could be all I needed to redeem me from speculative ideas and self-doubt. Abu Kasim's commonsense, the one or two favours that he would undoubtedly request from me, would quickly bring me back to the real world.

I went straight to Souk al-Bazerkhan where I found him seated in front of his shop, sipping coffee with admiring fellow merchants. I took Abu Kasim aside and invited him to join me on my walk. With no hesitation and in no time he was ready, leaving his shop to the care of 'Ali, the young coffee-boy and shop assistant he himself once was; but being no fool, he indicated by a movement of the head to one of the merchants that he should keep an eye on the boy and the shop.

Outside the walls a mulberry plantation dotted with a few habitations, mostly farms, spreads over a hill which gently stretches down to the sea. On the way, mulberry trees give way to cactus, wild fig trees and sand. Close to the sea is the Santiyeh cemetery, which we speedily passed, heading towards Ras-Beirut.

Feeling tired, Abu Kasim requested a halt. We sat on one of the fallen columns strewn along the beach. Those columns, and other remains of buildings, go back to ancient times, when the city was much bigger than it is now.

The city appeared even smaller when seen from afar by the infinite sea and at the foot of the mountains crowned with snow – a most majestic backdrop. All of a sudden my worries and doubts disappeared. I felt at peace with myself and paid more attention to Abu Kasim's talk. To my surprise, his discourse had a more elevated significance than I had expected.

'Remember,' he said, 'when we were both very young and very poor. One day my father sent me to fetch drinking water from 'Ain al-Karawiya (a spring much used by the Beirutis). On my way back, I dropped and broke the filled earthenware jug, much too heavy for me at my age. The pain from the thrashing I received is of course all gone, but I cannot ever forget the bitterness I felt, and I still feel, for having been unjustly punished.

'Now that I am rich, I want to prevent the same injustice befalling today's youth. What I have in mind is to set up a *wakf* (charitable endowment) which will consist of a shop in the property I own in the heart of the city. This shop will be full of all sorts of earthenware jugs. Whenever a boy, a girl or a poor person brings to the shop a broken jug, it will be replaced by a brand-new one.

'That is an idea which came to me this morning after prayer and I had in mind to discuss it with you at the first opportunity. The invitation to join you for a walk this very day is certainly no coincidence. It is God's will that the matter should proceed without delay.'

Abu Kasim looked at me and read appreciation and praise in my eyes. Encouraged by these signs he proceeded: 'Kasim, as you know, is of age now; but what you do not know, because I never mentioned it to you, is that I do not believe he is as good-hearted as I expected him to be. He gets his shrewdness from his mother; besides, he does not really know what it means to be poor and helpless. I suspect that the moment I disappear from this world, Kasim will seek to cancel the *wakf*. I want you to take all necessary legal measures so that he will not succeed if he ever tries.'

I reassured Abu Kasim by telling him that there is a legal stratagem which will protect the *wakf* not only from greed but also from any change of heart that he may himself experience. I outlined that device as follows: 'As the endower of the *wakf* you will appoint yourself and a person of confidence as co-administrators. As soon as the *wakf* is constituted, you will claim against your co-administrator that you have changed your mind and wish to cancel the *wakf* in accordance with the teaching of Abu Hanifa al-Na'man, who did not deem a *wakf* as binding, especially when the property constituted as a *wakf* is part of a joint estate.

'The co-administrator will resist such a claim on the grounds that the two Companions of Abu-Hanifa, Imam Abu Yusif and Imam Muhammad, did consider the setting up of a *wakf* as final and binding, whether or not it is in regard to a joint estate. I will rule on the dispute in accordance with the Companions' view, and your *wakf* will be safe from future pretence or claim.'

When we went back to the city we were both satisfied, Abu Kasim because he had found the solution to an immediate problem, I because the distant view of the seat of my worries had reduced those worries to their real dimensions.

. . . IT IS NOT OFTEN I find myself short of legal arguments. On the other hand, the case which actually puzzles me could not be counted among the routine disputes I normally oversee. It all started with those damned Frenchmen who rented a piece of land in the vicinity of the city and erected a silk-reeling factory on it. Their industry requires a lot of water, which they made available to themselves from a well they dug in the rented property. After a few weeks, their neighbours complained that they were deprived of the water they had normally used in the past. That is not a contested matter but astonishingly it is irrelevant to the resolution of the case. Apparently the French owners had sought solid legal advice, and their representative presented his arguments in defence of keeping the well open in a way which cannot be easily challenged. He rightly said that according to Abu Hanifa's teaching, underground water is owned by no one. He illustrated that principle with the classical – and in this case relevant – example of an imaginary Zaid, who used to benefit from water extracted from beneath his property until the time his neighbour, an imaginary 'Amr, dug a well in his property, which was on higher ground. As a result, all the water was retained by 'Amr. Zaid had no action against him, for underground water is the property of no one.

I cannot bring myself to rule in favour of the French owners. Foreigners have done a lot of harm to the community. Not only are they active in all walks of life; more dangerously, they help to destroy the fabric of our society.

By extending their protection and favour to the *dhimmis*, the latter become more prosperous by the day. Their arrogance will soon have no limits. It is enough that they behave like savages in their Mountains; here in the city, where they have flocked from their backward villages in search of peace and new business opportunities, we have to make them understand their real status.

I went to see the *Mufti*, Sheikh Ahmed, to discuss this irritating case. Needless to say, the French Consul had already had a word with him. I wonder why the Consul did not come to see me. Does he believe that the *Mufti* can give me orders? How ill-informed these foreigners can sometimes be.

We discussed the case but failed to find any way out of the unsatisfactory solution of the Hanafi school, whose teaching is the sole official teaching of the Empire. Sheikh Ahmed is a learned man who keeps in his library law books other than those by Hanafi authors. In a Maliki law treatise, it is said that Imam Malik does not allow a person to dig a well in his own property when such a well will decrease the volume of water of his neighbour's well; but that is Imam Malik, whose teaching cannot be followed here.

I left the *Mufti*'s house very disappointed. For a moment I even wondered whether Sheikh Ahmed had been persuaded by the French Consul not to inconvenience the French owners of the silk-reeling factory.

It was already dark and I could scarcely see my way in the narrow alleys. I was lost in deep thought and bumped into a passer-by. It was Abu Kasim. No, it was destiny. 'Abu Khalid,' he said, joking, 'were you at the story-teller's? Were you listening to the tale of 'Antar and 'Abla?'

I cut the jesting short and shared with Abu Kasim my concern. He immediately put himself in a serious mood and needed only a few seconds before he came up with a practical solution. He expounded his plan as follows: 'All we have to do is to talk to the owner of the property rented to the Frenchmen. If they have dug the well without his permission, the simplest way of dealing with the problem would be for the landlord to require the closure of the well and that will be the end of the matter.

'As it happens, I know that owner, Abu Zuhair. He will certainly testify that he never gave his tenants permission to dig the ground of his property. First thing in the morning I will see him, and in no time the well will be closed.'

. . . THE WELL in the ground of the silk-reeling factory will not be closed. Abu Kasim was informed by Abu Zuhair that he had sold the property to the Frenchmen. Vendor and purchasers had not yet come to me in order to bring evidence of the transaction, but soon they will. I will have no alternative except to bear witness to the transaction and as a consequence no one could ever challenge the Frenchmen's right to draw as much water as they want from their well. I feel discouraged. Abu Kasim, never short of new ideas and stamina, did not concede defeat. He told me that with Abu Zuhair's assistance he will try to entice away the workers at the silk-reeling factory, although they were engaged by the Frenchmen for a fixed period of time.

Yesterday Abu Kasim was so sure of himself. He was utterly convinced that the well would be sealed off in no time and I shared his optimism. We were both presumptuous; we took things for granted instead of putting them in the hands of God.

*Nor say of anything, 'I shall be sure to do so
and so tomorrow,' without adding, 'so please
God'.*

Qur'an, s.XVIII, 23, 24

. . . HAVING SOUGHT and obtained my permission, Umm Khalid,
'Aisha and Khadijah, accompanied by our young boy servant,
went to Abu Kasim's store to get material for new dresses.
Next they visited Mariam, their Jewish dressmaker, in a
nearby workshop. They found her frightened and alarmed.
She told them that an ominous incident had occurred that
morning which might have dangerous consequences for her
and her people. An Austrian Jew and a local merchant had a
dispute about the price of some goods provided by the former
to the latter. Their dispute degenerated into abusive language
on either side, although it was the Austrian who foolishly tried
to intimidate his opponent and resorted to cursing our pure
religion.

The merchant could not stand that outrage and appealed to
his fellow Muslims to avenge the insulted religion. An angry
crowd started to gather near the Austrian's residence. The
Austrian Consul was summoned. He saw the danger and,
before the crowd completely surrounded the place, called in
the aid of the military, who conducted the Austrian to the
Governor's palace amidst the imprecations of the infuriated
populace, who were closing in.

In the afternoon Mr Saba knocked on my door. He was
escorted by a few armed men and invited me to accompany
him to the Pasha to assist in calming down the crowd, who
were now gathered at the palace's door. On our way, Mr Saba
informed me that the Austrian Consul had sought his aid to
prevent a catastrophe. He, in turn, had turned to me for the
same elevated objective.

When we arrived at the palace, the enraged crowd made it
plain that they intended to kill the offender and warned us not
to try to prevent justice being done. Fear penetrated my heart

and nearly paralysed my movements. Mr Saba was up to the volatile situation. He talked to the crowd, displaying the assurance allowed by his privileged status, and calmed them down. I knew this was only temporary and seized the occasion of that respite to require that the offended party be summoned to the palace. I was sure that only a reconciliation between the parties could avoid dramatic developments.

Until then I had not even heard the name of that party, but when Abu Malik appeared before As'ad Pasha I felt relieved. Abu Malik is a reasonable man and a true believer; he would listen to our appeasing arguments.

Before long we convinced Abu Malik that it was the implied command of Allah's Shadow on Earth (the Sultan) to defuse the situation, which could be achieved only by his reconciliation with the foreigner. Mr Saba and the Austrian Consul promised him a number of business advantages, but only if he were accommodating.

Soon the Austrian Consul, Mr Saba, Abu Malik and myself were at the palace door. Abu Malik told the crowd that the whole matter was a misunderstanding and that the foreigner never intended to insult our sublime religion. He asked the people there to disperse, which they reluctantly did.

. . . 'AISHA is such a good-hearted girl. Once more she proved it to me this morning. She was worried that Mariam, the Jewish dressmaker, might still be in anguish on account of yesterday's dramatic episode. 'Aisha asked permission to pay her a visit and reassure her. Anyhow, she told me she had to go in the direction of Mariam's workshop, for she intended to exchange a piece of material bought from Abu Kasim as its colour was not to her liking any more. I allowed her to leave the house, accompanied by her sister and the servant.

Rabiʻ al-Awwal 1259 (March 1843)

A Jesuit priest before the council; Abu Kasim
repudiates his wife; the Qadi *visits the*
dragoman; a comet in the sky . . .

This morning I attended a session of the *majlis* at the Governor's palace. The case that we, the twelve members of the Council, had to examine was one of those instances which show how very pushy and arrogant the infidels can be the moment they feel they might have an edge.

Already under Egyptian rule, and then after the promulgation of the *hatt-i sharif*, missionaries, priests, and charlatans have swamped the region. American missionaries, the Russian Consul, the Methodists, and the Jesuits have established in Beirut some eight schools besides those schools started by local Catholic and Greek Orthodox priests.

I am not against the propagation of education among men, but the preaching of religions other than the rightful one should not be tolerated. We should not believe for a moment that foreign schools are here for our own benefit; they are but platforms for the spread of nefarious influences.

Is it not enough that the consuls interfere with the authorities in all matters, however small they may be? Now we also have to put up with the creation of unconforming indigenous forces. The people are angry and the authorities should be wary of that. It is my duty and the duty of the other members of the Council to contain popular discontent.

All these ideas rushed into my head on my way to the palace. They were prompted by the fact that a French Jesuit priest was

39

summoned to appear before the *majlis*, having committed two material violations of the law in relation to a property the Jesuits own just outside the walls to the east of the city. The property consists of a house erected on a large piece of land. I was told that the Jesuit who bought that property – a certain Father Abu Mansur – had encouraged the Mountains' uprising against the Great Emir, whose alliance with Ibrahim Pasha was doomed.

After the victory of our great Sultan over the Eygptians, Abu Mansur felt that the sympathy he had earned from the authorities and the principles heralded in *hatti-i sharif* allowed him to buy the property in question with no need for a *firman*. This he did, and the authorities turned a blind eye to the liberty he had taken. When Abu Mansur left the country, he was replaced by another priest who, encouraged by his pre-decessor's impunity, started ringing the bell of his church and expanding the construction erected on the property without any permission.

The Governor sent out a janissary to put an immediate end to these transgressions, but it was also felt that the *majlis* should deal with the matter once and for all. Hence the convocation of the new priest at today's session.

While on my way to the palace I wondered whether the priest would appear before us, because I had heard that the French Consul advised him not to. The Consul considers the *majlis* as lacking the jurisdiction to deal with cases which involve a French national – French nationals and indeed all foreign nationals being under the sole jurisdiction of consular tribunals.

As soon as I entered the Council's ante-room I saw two individuals whom I assumed were there in connection with the case. One was wearing local costume and the other a black frock-coat and black hat similar to those worn by the Polish and Russian Jews who pass through the region on their way to Jerusalem. Obviously the Jesuit did not listen to the French Consul's advice. That could only be to the advantage of his case.

When the two men entered the Council's room we discovered to our astonishment that both spoke perfect Arabic. The one wearing the frock-coat presented himself as Father Blanc and produced a *firman* which said, in substance, that the Jesuits were given permission to teach, preach and open schools in any part of the Empire without fear of opposition or hindrance from anyone.

The *firman* was handed round from one member to the other. After perusing it, I explained to the priest that the permissions contained in the *firman* did not include ringing a church bell or expanding buildings. I could not refrain from adding that if he was ordered to appear before us it was not because of an initiative on our part, but because the Council had received several complaints from other Christian quarters.

Father Blanc gracefully agreed that the old *firman* was silent about the matters which brought him before the Council. That *firman* was, however, not all he could produce in his defence. There was a new *firman*, obtained by his companion, whom he introduced as Brother Henri.

Brother Henri explained to us with great modesty that he had just arrived from Istanbul, where he had stayed a few months to pay his respects to 'Izzet Pasha, the Great Vizier, whom he, as a doctor, had tended and nursed when he was wounded during the campaign against the Egyptians. The Great Vizier had honoured him with his friendship and a *firman* appointing him as his personal doctor.

These were impressive credentials which immediately changed the Council's mood. We all knew that the new *firman*, like the old one, was not concerned with church bells and new constructions, but we did not wish to alienate the Jesuits' eminent protector. On the other hand, the Jesuits appeared to be sensible men. Hence the whole atmosphere was for conciliation.

A compromise was struck. The priests promised not to ring the bell any more and not to expand their existing buildings; the Council promised nothing, but it was plainly understood that it would not order the demolition of what was already built.

. . . You should show them kindness and deal justly with them. Allah loveth those who deal justly.

Qur'an, s. LX, 8

. . . ABU KASIM came to see me in a great state. It was to tell me that he had repudiated his wife by pronouncing three times a statement of divorce. Umm Kasim had immediately left town for Tripoli, where she has relatives.

The announcement was no surprise to me, yet Abu Kasim's agitated behaviour puzzled me. The divorce was an event expected by all who know Abu Kasim and certainly it has been on his mind for some time. Why, then, was he showing such a surprising agitation?

Soon the speculation was over; Abu Kasim was frightened of the repercussions for his trade. The redoubtable Umm Kasim had threatened to denounce him to the British Consul for having cheated his correspondent in Manchester regarding a delivery of fabrics allegedly damaged by sea water.

This was no insignificant matter and if proven – Abu Kasim's state was already a hint of guilt – could lead to his *abattellement*. '*Abattellement*' is derived from the Arabic verb *batil* (cancel, annul) and is a formidable weapon in the hands of European consuls. Whenever a foreign merchant is dissatisfied with a native's behaviour in relation to a business matter, he may summon him to appear before the consul of the merchant's country. Whether he complies or not with the summons is irrelevant. The consul examines the case and if convinced of its merit, he orders the boycott of the native and his merchandise. The decree of the boycott is notified to all European consuls in town and abroad; as a result, the boycotted native is driven to bankruptcy.

I promised Abu Kasim to talk to Mr Saba and get an assurance that the denunciation of a spurned woman will not be heeded.

. . . 'I KNEW that was going to happen.' With these words, Umm Khalid greeted me, and carried on: 'Umm Kasim has got what she deserved. How many times have I told her to behave properly with Abu Kasim and not to show him disdain – especially in front of other people. She is such a lovely person but she could not listen to reason when it came to her own interests. Now look what has befallen her.'

Umm Khalid has a strong predilection for hindsight. Whenever an event takes us by surprise, she will say without any hesitation, 'I told you so,' and then she would be right, for she always expects the worst.

Being certain that Umm Kasim must have given her all the details of the events which precipitated her repudiation, I asked to be told them.

Apparently Abu Kasim was in a bad mood when he came back home yesterday evening. Umm Kasim was not in and the dinner was not ready. Back from visiting a neighbour, she was met with his vehement reproaches. She foolishly retorted, 'I am not a slave and I am not accustomed to being in the service of anybody, unlike some.'

Abu Kasim could not bear to be reminded of his past duties as a coffee-boy. He became livid, stood up very slowly and solemnly repudiated her. Umm Kasim left the room, grumbling threats.

What a sad state of affairs this is. It could have been easily averted had Abu Kasim been more firm with Umm Kasim when she was under his *'usma* (care and control). A lifetime's leniency had ended with an extreme and radical decision in a moment of anger.

. . . AS PROMISED I went to see Mr Saba and for the first time entered his house, located near the port. The proximity of the sea is extremely unhealthy and I was surprised that an educated man – as Mr Saba indeed is – should choose such a site. His interest in the traffic of the port and the sea must have determined his choice; there is no other explanation.

From the street, and through a small and low-lying door, I entered a vast courtyard paved with marble. Here, in good weather, visitors are received under the fig trees and the lemon trees, allowing the chatter of their conversation to mix with the murmur of the running water. This time of the year was not suitable for staying outdoors, so I was ushered into a large room with a marbled floor almost entirely concealed beneath precious Persian carpets. The walls were panelled with cedar wood up to the height of a standing man.

The first part of the room is lower than the rest by one step and the two parts are separated by an elegantly carved banister. Two slaves stood in the lower part of the room, with coffee and pipes to hand.

The moment Mr Saba saw me he stood up and advanced towards me, enquiring about my health and complimenting me. I reciprocated his civilities and we sat together cross-legged on a settee hardly above the ground. The settee was covered with a beautiful *kilim* and engulfed in heaps of rich-looking cushions. Mrs Saba honoured me by appearing in the room. We were offered almonds and honey cakes, together with lemonade served in fine glasses. Then followed the usual coffee and pipes.

The customs of these native Christians are amazing; their women cover their faces in the street but not at home in front of strangers. Mrs Saba had milky-white skin and sparkling black, almond-shaped eyes. She was dressed in a short embroidered vest, baggy trousers and a large silk belt from which the inlaid hilt of an ornamental dagger peeped out. An astonishing piece of her clothing caught my eye: the pair of tiny red slippers she wore. I promised myself to search the whole Souk al-Sarame (the shoe market) for a pair of slippers like that for Umm Khalid to wear for me at home.

After Mrs Saba had retired, I revealed the object of my visit and expressed the hope that no trouble would befall Abu Kasim. Abu Kasim was no stranger to Mr Saba and that made it easy for him to accept to plead his case with the Consul as best he could.

When my interlocutor told me that he in turn would like me to do him a favour I felt glad because I did not wish to remain in his debt for long, and also because it could mean only that the intercession on behalf of Abu Kasim would necessarily succeed. The following is exactly what my friend told me.

'Two years ago, as you perfectly know, Mount Lebanon was in turmoil. Christians and Druzes were at each others throats. It was only owing to the Sublime Porte's intervention and that of some European countries that the slaughter came to an end. The Emirs Shehab were rightly seen as partly responsible for the trouble, and their removal from office helped bring back peace. In truth, what also calmed down the situation was the partition of the Mountains into two *kaymacamiyyat*, one for the Druzes and one for the Christians.

'France is unhappy about the arrangement and sees it as a way of depriving the Maronites – the religious community it protects – from the right of administering the entire Mountains. France is above all worried about the Druzes' getting out from under its own influence.

'Its envoys and missionaries, together with the Maronite Patriarch, intrigue to have back in power the Great Emir Bashir, or failing him, his son Emir Amin. Fortunately, not all Maronite notables have the same views. I am advised by my Consul, Colonel Rose, that the heads of the powerful Khazen family have addressed a petition to the Pope, imploring him to prevent the clergy from interfering in the politics of the Mountains.

'My Government is in favour of keeping the actual status quo and will do whatever necessary to that end. What I would like from you is to be introduced to your neighbour, Sheikh Abu 'Abbas, who has a certain influence in the Druzes'

Mountain. His assistance is needed for matters which will enhance peace. But we will discuss all of that when we see him.'

Mr Saba's discourse left me a little worried. What was requested of me was to meddle with political matters. The reassuring aspect, however, was that it was nothing directed against the politics of our Master the Sultan.

I promised to arrange a meeting with Abu 'Abbas as soon as convenient.

. . . YESTERDAY AFTERNOON when I left the dragoman's residence it was already dark. I wandered in the street, hardly being able to see my way and having no particular design in mind. I felt sad and gloomy for no apparent reason. In fact, I knew there must be some reason I did not want to admit to myself, but eventually I would have to, for if there is one trait of character I have always hated, it is definitely self-delusion. I have no gift for self-delusion, and gift it is. People imbued with their own self-importance and endowed with that characteristic not only end up being convinced of their superiority but often succeed in convincing others. Of course, it is much easier to attain this second stage with the aid of wealth. In reality there would be no need to spend any money; it would be enough that others know it was there. Without even showing its colour, money buys you knowledge and wisdom enough to squander.

Listen to a wealthy person speak. His delivery is slow, he articulates fully, keeping his voice low and restrained. He does not fear interruption and he could take all the time in the world; nobody would ever consider snatching from him his part in the conversation, however insipid it may be. Others less fortunate speak quickly for fear of being interrupted or, worse, ignored. I suddenly realized that my gloominess could be due to jealousy. Am I resentful of Mr Saba's luxurious residence and his many servants and slaves in attendance? I do not think so. After all, I have never envied Abu Kasim, who is probably much wealthier than the dragoman, although much less ostentatious and pathetically unhappy in life. That is it. It is not Mr Saba's wealth which I have resented; rather it is the happiness and contentment which emanate from his hearth and home. He and his wife are one and I have realized in my heart that I could never be of one mind and one soul with Umm Khalid.

How could I let her share every moment in my life and be privy to my inner thoughts? I surely cannot make her the witness of my sorrow and the partner of my joy, otherwise she would end up by considering herself my equal. I have to accept that and continue to live a solitary inner life, whatever happens to me.

Having touched the reason of my unhappiness, I felt much better and returned home. My young servant, who was waiting for me, informed me that Umm Khalid had retired to bed but had left him instructions to warn her the moment I arrived. I told him to go to bed, which he did gratefully.

I climbed the few stairs which lead to Umm Khalid's night recess and lay alongside her. When I approached her that night, I could not erase from my mind the image of Mrs Saba's red slippers.

. . . WE WERE ALL frightened by the appearance of a star in the sky. It was an enormous ball with a tail and it stood close to the sun. We first took it for a thin cloud illuminated by the reflections of the setting sun, but soon we realized it was not that but a terrifying phenomenon.

The whole city's population stood on the houses' flat roofs watching in silence. One could see from the expressions in their eyes that people had one question in mind: is this the end of the world?

I must confess that the inexplicable celestial mani-festation terrified me at first, but then I recited God's words:

47

It is He who created the Night and the Day,
and the sun and the moon; all the celestial
bodies swim along, each in its rounded course.

Qur'an, s. XXI, 33

and peace returned to my heart.

. . . KHADIJAH, my fourteen-year-old favourite daughter, rested her head on my shoulder and complained, 'I would like so much to take advantage of this beautiful day and go with you for an outing to an open place, to a café by the sea, for example. For ages we have not had a moment together; we miss your wise conversation and the benefit of your advice.'

Who could have resisted the cleverness of her tongue and the innocence which emanated from her eyes? I did not. It was Friday, I did not have much to do and the weather was really glorious.

'Tell everybody to get ready. We will go to Abu Darwish's,' I said. Abu Darwish runs a café for families by the sea, overlooking the port.

Half an hour later, I took Khalid by the hand and we made our way in the direction of the port, followed by Umm Khalid, 'Aisha and Khadijah, themselves followed by our young servant. On the way I avoided the Greek quarter, full of cafés unsuitable for decent people. Instead we went through a street that has become the favourite haunt among money-changers and money-lenders, as well as the place where most consulates have been established.

Finally we reached our destination. When we emerged from the dirty, dark and narrow streets of the city, the open space of the port seemed more dazzling.

Several sailing ships, fishing boats and one steamer rode at anchor in the roadstead, which is closed by a tongue-like salience protecting the waters from eastern winds. The whole of that salience and the neighbouring hills are covered with the riches of vegetation: mulberry trees dominate, while carob trees, fig trees, citrus trees and a number of other plants struggle to make room for themselves.

Further away, on the first slopes of the mountains, is a forest of the blessed olive trees and in the background rise the mountains, crowned with snow. It is that snow, white as *laban*, which gave the mountains the name of Loubnan.

The quay was full of people bustling around. Small boats loaded with local goods, and other goods from faraway places such as Cairo, Damascus and Baghdad, shuttled between the shore and the ships at anchor. Camels, donkeys and mules waited patiently to be loaded or to be relieved of their burdens.

Abu Darwish's café stands on a wooden platform which dominates the beach and is supported by columns. We were about to enter one of the small cabins which provide adequate private quarters where wives and daughters can safely lift their veils, when I saw Abu Kasim, his three sons, and 'Ali, his coffee-boy. I rushed my women into the cabin and went to Abu Kasim. I did not stay long with him, for I remembered Khadijah's complaint and wish for my company.

Coffee, water-ices and a *narghile* were brought to the cabin, where we all sat comfortably on a mat of rushes, our faces turned towards the sea, which we could see through the cabin's opening. The repetitive ebb and flow of the waves fascinated us and reduced us, even Khadijah, to silent meditators. 'Aisha was absorbed in deep contemplation, Umm Khalid drew on her *narghile* with no word uttered and Khalid was busy eating his water-ice. After a while, I remembered Khadijah's earlier praises and I felt compelled to break the silence and say something suited to the occasion. I recited:

> *'If the ocean were ink wherewith to write out*
> *the words of the Lord, sooner would the ocean*
> *be exhausted than would the words of my Lord,*
> *even if we added another ocean like it, for its aid.'*
>
> Qur'an, s. XVIII, 109

Why is it that 'Aisha – she who used to be full of life and joy – stared at me with lacklustre eyes?

. . . I AM REALLY WORRIED about 'Aisha. In the early part of the day she, her sister and our servant went to Mariam's, the dressmaker's workshop, for a fitting. When they came back 'Aisha was pale and uncommunicative. She went straight to her mattress, refusing to take any food or liquid. She even turned down a cup of hot orange-flower water prepared by her mother. In the afternoon she was still in the same state and I decided to send for Dr Caporelli. Dr Caporelli is an Italian doctor who made Beirut his home during the Eygptian occupation and remained after their withdrawal. Very knowledgeable and helpful, he attends to the Pasha's health and looks after all the city's dignitaries. He refuses to take any money from them and what he takes from the others is reasonable. Eminent and rich people are very fond of him and praise his art and his humanitarian nature; common people are prepared to sell or pledge whatever valuable asset they may have to be entitled to his diagnoses and receive his treatment. Dr Caporelli always dresses like the Europeans, lest he be mistaken for any of those local charlatans who roam the country and dispense the same phoney remedies for all sorts of ailments.

The moment Dr Caporelli answered my call, I took him to 'Aisha, who was tended by her mother. Over her blouse's sleeve he felt her pulse and in perfect Arabic he asked permission to examine her tongue. I gave my assent by nodding. 'Aisha lifted part of her veil, just enough to reveal her mouth and extend her tongue.

'Nothing to worry about,' said the good doctor. 'For two days feed her with *laban* but nothing else and give her one of these pills with a little water four times a day. All bad vapours will soon disappear. In the unlikely case that she does not improve, I will then have to bleed her or to apply leeches.'

That was enough for 'Aisha to declare that she was feeling better already.

... SHEIKH ABU 'ABBAS RECEIVED me and the dragoman in the *manzul* adjoining the house he had rented when, with his family, he escaped the bloodshed which drained the Mountains. His dress was that of a Druze *'aqil* (a person who knows the intricacies of the Druzes' religion). His twisted white turban was rolled around a brimless cap and he wore a woollen *'aba* with alternating white and black stripes. His demeanour was dignified and imposing.

Once the customary compliments were exhausted, Mr Saba gave a brief account of the political events of the moment before embarking upon the real aim of our visit. For the wisdom and foresight they entail, I have reported below and as exactly as possible his words.

'The clashes between Druzes and Christians make it unthinkable to give control of the whole Mountains to either a Maronite Emir or a Druze one. The recent murderous events have unleashed suspicion, fanaticism and fear. You must have heard that a few days ago a seventy-year-old Maronite priest was slain by his relatives while he was on his way to pay an innocent visit on an *'aqil* friend of his. The unfortunate priest did not heed the ban on such relationships, a ban imposed by the secret committee of Deir al-Kamar.

'My Government was, and remains, fully aware of the new circumstances which have arisen out of tragic political and bloody events. That explains why it has strongly favoured the partition of the Mountains into two districts, one for each community.

'The two *kaymacamiyyat* are now a reality. Given time, the few drawbacks that have emerged following the implementation of the new organization will be remedied. I regret to say that some quarters are unwilling to concede that necessary respite. On the contrary, they do everything in their power to destroy what we have painfully achieved. France is one of those opposed to the division of the Mountains into two districts. France wants to reinstate the Christian Bashir Shehab or one of his sons as the Emir of all Mount Lebanon. The Maronite clergy and the Catholic missionaries work towards that end, which would bring more sorrow if it were ever achieved.'

Abu 'Abbas was listening intently. He then took advantage of a pause to proffer: 'You both greatly honoured me and this house by your visit and by taking me into your confidence. The great nations' designs and plans as expounded by Mr Saba give a just measure of one's powerlessness and a clear warning not to exceed one's limits. How can your humble servant influence in any way the events prompted by the great nations, if that is God's will?'

Sheikh Abu 'Abbas's protests of powerlessness were expected. Besides being genuine, they incited the dragoman to disclose what he had in his mind and what kind of assistance he was seeking. Mr Saba grasped the situation well and became more explicit.

'Sheikh Abu 'Abbas, modesty is one of your many qualities. Indeed we are the submissive instruments of the Creator. Our conscience is our guide, as well as evidence of His will, yet if we do not partake in performing what our conscience dictates, more blood will be shed and your people will be subjected to Bashir's political and religious tyranny. You have asked what you can do. Certainly you can do a lot. You are a man of influence among the Yazbaki circle and among the *'uqqal*. Work to consolidate with them the actual status quo in the Mountains and allow British and American preachers to establish their bases there. Let them bring more instructions to your youth and give them the opportunity to thwart seditious plans.

'For your information, the Janbalati party has seen the benefit of that policy and agreed to follow it. One of our frigates will soon take the youngest of the Janbalats to

England, at the request of the highest religious authorities, for him to pursue his education with them.'

Thereafter we talked about other matters, but obviously Sheikh Abu 'Abbas was satisfied with what he had heard.

Rabi' al-akhar 1259 (April 1843)

Getting a new garment cures illness;
resolution of the case of the disputed
orchard; murder of the magic lantern's showman;
a journey to Sidon . . .

. . . Could it be possible that a new garment has the power to cure illness? I witnessed just such a wonder when Mariam brought home the garment she had sewn for 'Aisha. The moment 'Aisha put it on, she claimed to be better and left the mattress where she had lain for over two days.

In no time 'Aisha and Khadijah were playing together like the two little girls they are, and I watched them with a feeling of great tenderness. One day I will marry them to two decent men and they will be under the care and custody of their respective husbands. I will feel much more relaxed when that happens, knowing that they are no longer my responsiblity. I have enough to do with Khalid's education and the preparation of his future. Until now I have been unable to detect where his interest lies. When I teach him the Qur'an he tires quickly and complains about dizziness. Umm Khalid pulls him away from me with reproach in her eyes for my insensitivity and lack of awareness of his young age.

I promised myself to ask his teacher of grammar and syntax, *muallem* Shibli, how his pupil is doing.

. . . Sheikh Bshara al-Khuri reappeared before my court more than one month after he had filed the lawsuit on behalf of the Emir Shehab against Jebraeel Mussa, the occupier of the orchard which is claimed by the former as his property.

Sheikh Bshara was accompanied neither by the defendant nor by his attorney. In principle, one condition essential for the furtherance of legal proceedings was therefore missing. Nevertheless, Sheikh Bshara handed over to me a written *fatwa* from the *Mufti* Sheikh Ahmed al-Radwan which was intended to encourage me to proceed with the case in the absence of both the defendant and his attorney. The *fatwa* said that I could appoint a legal representative who would stand for the defendant and that I could proceed with my inquiry about the moral standing of the witnesses in the absence of the party against whom they have testified, because the objective of the *tazikya* is to establish the witnesses' reliability to the judge and not to that party.

Armed with the *Mufti*'s *fatwa*, I decided to conduct the procedure of *tazkiya*. The reliability of each of Sheikh Bshara's witnesses was attested by two other witnesses stating under oath, 'He is reliable and one can be satisfied.'

At once I summoned the defendant's attorney to appear before me. He complied but claimed that his client had dismissed him. I appointed him legal representative of Jebraeel Mussa and ruled against the latter, finding that the orchard belongs to the Emir Shehab and that his usurpation should immediately cease.

. . . FOR SEVERAL DAYS most of my time has been taken up by a murder case. Murder is not common in our city – praise be to God. This one was most appalling. Its victim was Juan the Spaniard, a magic lantern's showman who used to tour near and distant provinces, returning to Beirut every now and then to perform in front of a lost-in-wonder audience. A few days ago he gave a performance in one of the cafés by the sea and went back to his rented room in the *khan*. In the morning he was discovered immersed in a blood bath, his throat cut from ear to ear. No money was found in his room, although it was known that his performance the evening before, a Thursday, was attended by a packed audience, which meant that the takings were as high as ever.

Suspicions arose against a sailor from Malta who had attended the unfortunate Spaniard's last show and who was lodged in the same *khan*. The Maltese's room was searched by the police and a knife stained with blood was discovered hidden under the floor. Traces of blood were also found on his clothes and an unusually large number of piastres in his pocket. Confronted with the incriminating evidence, the Maltese confessed his crime and was thrown into gaol.

The murderer being a British subject, the Governor summoned a meeting of the *majlis* and invited the British Consul to attend in order to decide the murderer's fate. The impressive and severe-looking Colonel Rose answered the Governor's invitation, accompanied by Mr Saba. They joined the *majlis*'s members already in session.

Colonel Rose said, and Mr Saba translated to the audience, 'My Government regrets that an atrocious crime was committed by one of its subjects against another European. Although one cannot but feel extremely sorry for the victim and his family, I thank God that no Ottoman subject was harmed in the process.

'The Most Gracious and Mighty Sultan has granted a British subject accused of a crime against a non-Ottoman subject the privilege of being tried by a British court. That generous concession, for which my Government is most grateful, is made in the Capitulations. I therefore ask that the Maltese be delivered, when I so request, to the skipper of one of Her Majesty's vessels, to be taken to England for trial.'

At this juncture Abu Ibrahim, one of the *majlis*'s members, intervened. Abu Ibrahim has a grudge against all Europeans for the reason that his silk manufacture is on the verge of closure because he is unable to compete in terms of prices with silk fabrics imported from Europe. He said, 'A crime was committed here and the accused should be tried here by the Pasha. Let me ask you, what would you say or do if the victim were one of us? Would you let the criminal escape our justice?'

Colonel Rose was quick to reply: 'The Mighty Sultan in his vast wisdom has foreseen the hypothetical case mentioned by Abu Ibrahim. Thus articles 24 and 42 of the Capitulations state that any British subject accused of the murder of a Turkish subject on Turkish territory must be tried by a joint Turkish and British tribunal on Turkish territory. I thank God once more that the Maltese's crime was not committed against any Turkish subject and I reiterate my request that the accused be delivered to me.'

The *majlis* was obviously impressed and convinced by the Consul's address. A resolution was taken and recorded in the minutes to the effect that the Maltese will stand trial in England.

A satisfied Colonel addressed the *majlis*: 'You will certainly not want me to thank you or congratulate myself for this resolution. Despite my poor Arabic and dreadful pronunciation, I would like to quote one of your sapient proverbs: Duty deserves no thanks.'

We were all beaming with pleasure. It is such a satisfaction to know that our language and culture could interest persons of rank and distinction who, in addition, modestly acknowledge the difficulty they have in touching on both.

The Consul pursued his address: 'The Maltese has confessed his crime and that confession will be enough to convict him in England, provided we establish to the satisfaction of the court and jury that the confession was obtained from him without pressure and without intimidation.

'I therefore propose that the Qadi Sheikh 'Abdallah record in writing the Maltese's confession and the circumstances in which it was made, in the presence of several witnesses, including Dr Caporelli and myself. That, I believe, will be sufficient to attest the validity and authenticity of the confession to the court.'

The *majlis* recorded a resolution in that direction.

. . . With the Consul, Dr Caporelli, six *shuhud al-hal* and the Court's clerk, I went to the gaol where the Maltese was imprisoned. The Palace's basement serves as a gaol so the guards of the Pasha can double as warders. The place gave me the shivers, although I knew that I was there on duty and for only an hour or two. My companions remained silent and I presume that they were as uneasy as I was.

We were conducted to the prisoner, who was chained to the wall and showed vast relief when he was told by Colonel Rose that he would be taken to England to be tried. Probably he welcomed the respite provided by the voyage. Otherwise I could not see why he should be so cheerful.

He was examined by Dr Caporelli, who confirmed that he did not detect traces of beating. I could have confirmed that myself with no need to examine the prisoner, who had already confessed and made the beating purposeless.

Then the prisoner was interrogated by the Consul, and the doctor translated the questions and answers for the records. The Maltese confessed his crime, but he went on to give details of how it happened, details which I found completely useless. The Consul, however, wanted every one of them recorded. At his request, the clerk put in writing that indeed the Maltese went to the Spaniard's room to rob him of the evening's takings, that the Spaniard woke up and charged at him with a knife, that he was able to fend off the attack and to take his own knife, with which he cut the Spaniard's throat.

The Consul asked whether a knife was found in the deceased's room. Nobody was able to tell. I, however, remarked that as part of my duties I would have to make an inventory of the deceased's estate. In a day or two I would be able to report to the Consul whether such a knife was among the Spaniard's belongings.

. . . The next day I decided to draw up the inventory of Juan's belongings. His room at the *khan* was bare of furniture except for a torn carpet stretched on the floor next to a double bag left wide open. Several books were scattered around the bag and in one corner I found what was the source of Juan's livelihood, the magic lantern and several glass plates bearing painted forms, shapes and scenes. I could find no knife, or any other weapon, in the room. When later on I mentioned this to the Consul, he requested a copy of the inventory.

I made a list of what was in the room and I assessed the value of each object. For a while everything will be kept in my custody in case any of the deceased's heirs appears and claims his share, otherwise everything will be sold by auction and the proceeds given to the *awkaf*, after deduction of costs.

It was relatively easy to assess the value of the blood-stained carpet, one large shawl, one shirt, one pair of trousers, two candles, one piece of soap and three small pieces of material used as towels. When it came to the magic lantern and its accessories, I was unable to put a price on them. I had never seen a similar instrument close up and I wonder whether in the whole Provinces one man who was able to make it work could be found. I decided to leave the matter aside for the time and I looked at the books on the floor.

They were all Arabic. Juan, who had spent all his adult life in the Provinces, was much more familiar with that language than with his mother tongue. One book was by al-'Amili on algebra, another one was on nature; there were two on astrology and one on astronomy. Astrology was not of any interest to me. I certainly do not believe that the movements of the planets and of the stars could influence our lives; that would be blasphemy. The sole Master of our destiny is God:

> To Him belongs the dominion of the heavens and the
> earth: it is He who gives life and death; and He
> has power over all things.
>
> Qur'an, s. LVII, 2

Astronomy, the scientific study of the objects that God has put in the sky, is something different. I would like to know

59

the movements of the stars and understand the reasons and purposes of the celestial phenomena. After all, our forefathers mastered astronomy and left us a considerable legacy on the matter. But where are their books? None of them is available here. People still believe that when the moon or the sun is eclipsed, it is because a dragon is about to swallow the disappearing star. When such a phenomenon is in process, people climb on their roof terraces, fire their rifles in the air and with all sorts of copper utensils produce the most dreadful of noises in order to scare the dragon and send it away.

I took the book on astronomy for myself, pledging to pay a fair price for it.

. . . IMMEDIATELY after performing the *salat al-fajr* (dawn prayer) I bade farewell to Khalid and the women, mounted a hired mule and rode towards Sayda through the city's south gate. With me rode the court's clerk and the muleteer, *raïs* Ismail, the trusted conveyor of the mail and small valuable articles intended for the inhabitants of the towns and villages of the south. Arrangements were made that we would reach Sayda by land – a journey which would take the whole day – and that I and the clerk, once our business was completed, would return by boat – a six-hour sail.

Sayda was my mother's town of birth. She left it for Beirut, never to return, at the age of sixteen, when she wedded my father. I never knew exactly why my father had adamantly refused to accompany her to the place of her childhood, or to allow her to go there on her own. It must have been something to do with his quarrel with her younger brother, my uncle, who pursued a lifestyle which my father could not tolerate. After my father's death, I promised to take her to Sayda, to the enchanted orchards of her youthful imagination. I was prevented from keeping my promise by her premature demise, which occurred two years ago, when the Creator took back His deposit – her pure soul – during an outbreak of plague.

'. . . those who have faith and work righteousness,
they are the Companions of the Garden; therein
shall they abide (for ever).'

Qur'an, s. II, 82

Half an hour after we left Bab al-Darkah (the south gate)
we entered a boundless pine forest. In between the trunks we
could see, on the right, white and reddish sandhills and
occasionally the sea, calm but nevertheless intimidating. At
one point when we had to climb a small elevation, we enjoyed
on our left a magnificent view of a sea of another kind, a vast
blue-green olive grove which extends as far as the eye can see
and expires at the feet of the range of Mount Lebanon.

When finally we came out of the pine forest, we followed
the sea-shore. Whenever the beach was sandy, we sensed the
mules' relief and satisfaction; when pebbly, their steps became
cautious and wary, calling our attention to more careful
riding.

A couple of hours before the *salat al-ʿasr* (afternoon prayer)
we reached the River Damoor and decided to get some rest at
the *khan* which stands by the old bridge. There we were served
coffee and ate the provisions that Umm Khalid had wisely
prepared for us, before resuming our journey.

Late in the afternoon we reached a desolate area which I
estimated to be two or three hours' ride from Sayda. Our guide
slowed down his mount until I drew level with him. Obviously
he needed a chat.

'You know,' said he, 'above us, up in the mountain of Djoun,
lived the *sitt* [Lady Hester Lucy Stanhope] who died not long
ago. She enjoyed supernatural powers and great wealth. Near
the end of her life her means dwindled and as a consequence
the number of her familiars diminished. She was about to
regain fortune and friends – only death was the quicker. Fate
can be so harsh.'

I have heard of the English lady and of her predicament
from an employee of the British consulate who was there

when the inventory of her estate was drawn up. Weary and unwilling to pursue a dialogue studded with philosophical thoughts, I gave our guide a nod of agreement with no word uttered. He understood the message and pressed his mule on to ride ahead of the party.

Just before sunset we arrived at our destination, and lodged in a *khan* overlooking the massive fortress which emerges from the water and is connected with the shore by a stony bridge.

Although exhausted, I decided to write the details of my journey while they were still fresh in my memory, before going to sleep.

. . . ONLY WHEN I read what I wrote yesterday did I realize that I have not said a word about the reason for my trip to Sayda.

In fact, I am not the only jurist who has made the journey. Here are gathered the *Mufti* of Damascus, the present and former *Muftis* of Beirut, and two well-respected scholars. We were all invited by the local Qadi to assist him in adjudicating a delicate case brought before his court at the Governor of Nablus's order, to secure fair justice which could not be attained there because the litigants are all persons of importance and able to lean equally on Nablus's magistrates.

In terms of facts, the case is a simple one: the attorney of a *wakf*'s trustee – the latter being the woman Hajji Safwat bint 'Ali Salameh – had given the entrusted property to a certain Ibrahim Mer'i in exchange for another property and a sum of money on the alleged ground, evidenced by witnesses, that the entrusted property was falling into ruins and the large amount of money needed for repair was unavailable.

Hajji Safwat, in her capacity as a principal and trustee, objected to the exchange, submitting that it was untrue that the entrusted property was dilapidated at the time of the exchange.

She also produced a *fatwa* issued by the *Mufti* of Damascus which said in substance that if, as a matter of actual fact, the entrusted property was not in the derelict state it was said to be in at the time of the exchange, then that exchange would be null and void. Hajji Safwat's witnesses – all very prominent and reliable people – gave evidence in favour of her account.

The Qadi of Sayda deliberated with those of us who were in attendance during the whole proceedings, and was about to order Ibrahim Mer'i to give back the entrusted property, when the latter claimed that there was another reason for the exchange. He expounded that the *dhimmi* Wehbeh Murad – a civil servant of Nablus's Treasury – had forcibly occupied part of the entrusted property, using it for his habitation, and that Murad's coercion was another ground justifying the exchange.

The Qadi commented that the matter of coercion was never raised before, that from the evidence provided Wehbeh Murad had paid rent for his lodging and in any event that *dhimmi* was not a person who could exercise coercion. As a result the Qadi invalidated the exchange involving the entrusted property.

. . . HAVING SPENT a second night in the *khan*, I decided to leave Sayda, for I had no other business and my uncle, my mother's brother, was out of town. So my clerk and I boarded a boat which was about to sail for Beirut. It was daybreak and a little chilly; I stayed under the canvas which was fixed up to protect travellers and cargo from the inclemency of the weather.

Rays of light filtering from behind the mountains spread rapidly over the gardens, the houses and the fortress's walls, driving darkness away and giving life to each and every object they touched, inexorably extending the territory conquered by lightness.

It was peaceful and blissful. Nostalgia for such a place hung around my mother her entire life. The amazing part was that she also kept vivid in her memory her father's stories about the barbaric cruelty of the ruler at the time of her childhood, but whenever she retold those stories it was as if Sayda was unconcerned and untarnished by the fall-out of human insanity. I must say that my mother was very young and over-indulged when she married my father and left for Beirut for good. That was the year Bonaparte besieged Acre.

Acre was then the seat of the Pashalik of Sayda and the Bosnian Ahmad Pasha al-Jazzar was appointed its ruler during the final quarter of the last century. He brought his people misery, fear, torture and death.

When I decided to study law, hoping that one day I could be appointed Qadi, my mother, who had developed a suspicious and guarded mind from her own experiences in life and also from the recollection of her father's stories, painted the following one for my sake, intending to warn me not to put my trust in anyone.

'Ahmad al-Jazzar relied for financial matters on his adviser the Jew *muallem* Haïm and for legal matters on the *Mufti*. Both men had a fair number of enemies and spent much of their time fending off devious plots intended for their downfall. The *Mufti* was a lazy person and relied heavily on his clerk, who did all his work. Every Thursday morning the clerk piled up in two stacks the petitions presented to the *Mufti* during the week; one stack for those petitions which should be approved by the *Mufti* and the other for those which should be rejected. Invariably the *Mufti* wrote the word "approved" or "rejected" and signed, following the clerk's grouping without even glancing at the petitions.

'The *Mufti*'s foes bribed the clerk, who slipped into the stack of petitions meant to be approved one petition which could not but be rejected because of the obvious violation of the *sharia* which it entailed. As was his custom, the *Mufti* blindly conformed to his clerk's arrangements and unwittingly approved the damning petition, which was immediately taken to al-Jazzar. He showed it to the *Mufti*, requiring explanation.

'Incapable of justifying his deed, the *Mufti* broke down and begged for a few days' grace to try to exonerate himself. He was given a day, and retired to his house, already in mourning for himself.

'*Muallem* Haïm heard of his predicament and went to offer

his help. Nothing humanitarian in that: both had the same enemies, and the downfall of one meant the weakening and eventual crash of the other.

'*Muallem* Haïm examined the incriminating petition for a few long minutes, then said, "Scratch out the word 'approved'." The *Mufti*, profoundly disappointed, replied, 'Is that your advice? If I follow it I should expect no mercy from our master, who would feel offended by such a childish attempt to hide my dreadful mistake!'

'*Muallem* Haïm smiled and retorted, "I do not expect you to scratch out the word 'approved' and to write 'rejected' instead. I expect you to rewrite 'approved'. You will draw the Pasha's attention to the scratching marks and he will undoubtedly be driven to believe that one of your enemies scratched your initial word 'rejected' and replaced it with the word 'approved'."

'Eventually the *Mufti* saved his neck and learned two lessons: to be more diligent, and not to rely on anyone.'

'. . . DO YOU REMEMBER, O Abu Khalid, the time of our youth, when we did not have any worries other than to make sure that we could eat our fill each day and get away with our pranks? More than once you shared with me the piece of bread, the portion of cheese or the few onions that your poor mother – God be merciful to her soul – used to provide you with for the day. Often I had nothing to eat, but your generous mind inevitably made me partake in your meal.'

In this manner Abu Kasim addressed himself to me. We were sitting in his house, smoking pipes and sipping one cup of coffee after another. I refrained from smiling because, unknown to Abu Kasim, I had always been aware that more than once he had succumbed to the temptation of forgoing his lunch for a more lasting object he had seen and coveted, being sure he would always be able to share the food I had. I have known that since childhood, but I never alluded to it, being too afraid to make him ashamed of himself. I decided to mention it now and see his reaction.

Abu Kasim affected not to have heard a word of what I said, and proceeded: 'I knew then that you were anxious to put into practice your goodness and your charitable inclinations; so, from time to time, I pretended to be unprovided with any food, just to give you the occasion to be benevolent.' He looked at me with a twinkle in his eye and we burst out laughing.

Unscrupulous, sure of himself and witty, that is how Abu Kasim could be described; that is how he had attracted the shy and unsure youth I was. With the passing years we developed a friendship, solid and lasting, the more so because we took different paths in life and never competed.

Abu Kasim resumed his talk: 'Look around you, my dear friend, notice the numerous carpets from Damascus, the *kilim* cushions, the opulent silver-studded chest and the beautiful weapons hanging on the wall. I made it. I am rich and respected. The Governor, who also benefits from the bounties that Allah in his munificence bestowed upon me, his slave, cannot refuse me a favour. Everyone knows that, so jealousy is restrained and marks of respect exaggeratedly increased.

'I have three sons and no daughter; and now I have no wife. I could not bear any longer Umm Kasim's disapproving attitude. With all the glaring success I enjoy, a side look from her made me uneasy. She was the only person capable of unsettling me and I could not bear it any more.

'You know, my dearest friend, that a man without a woman is like the player of the *'oud* (lute) without a musical instrument. I would like to strengthen our friendship even more; I would like to marry your daughter 'Aisha. Your conditions are mine.'

I must say I did not expect such a proposal, and it left me dumbstruck for a moment. When I could resume speaking, I said, 'We are the dearest of friends and the prospect of 'Aisha becoming part of your family enchants me. With a heart full of joy, I accept! I would like, however, to break the wonderful news to 'Aisha and to Umm Khalid, not immediately, but after a short while. We all need some time to get accustomed to the idea. You are aware of Umm Khalid's friendship with Umm Kasim – they are like two sisters; not to forget that 'Aisha used to call you Uncle and Umm Kasim, Auntie; and what about me? I will have to learn to be your father-in-law!'

We both giggled as we used to do ages ago.

Jumada al-oula 1259 (May 1843)

Conclusion of the silk-reeling-factory case;
protected dhimmi or Ottoman subject?; assault on the
Greek Orthodox bishop; case of the long-nosed neighbour;
'Aisha is advised of her pending marriage . . .

. . . I WAS GIVEN a *firman* which allows the French owners of the silk-reeling factory to acquire ownership of the land on which that factory stands. At the same time Abu Zuhair's attorney and the French owners' attorney came to my court to confirm and certify the conveyance of the property from the former to the latter.

I had no alternative but to be witness to a legal usurpation. I blamed myself for that and also for being the unwilling accomplice in a scheme which tends to rob our community of the return expected from an industry which was started long before foreign competition was brought to our lands. To make a deplorable situation worse, the *dhimmis* enrich themselves in the process owing to their connivance with their alien brothers in religion.

I wonder whether our great Sultan is aware of the baleful effects of his benevolence and graciousness. He has decreed that all his subjects are equal regardless of religion. Yet the result is the opposite of what was expected. The *dhimmis* have nearly taken over a commanding status and deprived us of our livelihoods.

I pray Allah that everything and everyone revert to their original position and place. That is something which is in the Sultan's power to do, and he should act now. I do not understand his leniency. Were he under a spell, special prayers could break that spell.

With the *firman* came a *fatwa* from the Grand *Mufti* of Istanbul, given to the owners of the silk-reeling factory through the medium of the French Ambassador to the Sublime Porte.

The opinion of such a person of rank was requested when the owners became aware of an underground activity which was trying to entice away their workers. The short but curt *fatwa* reads as follows: 'Assuming that (an imaginary) Zaid has employed (an imaginary) 'Amr to do a specific job during a given time and against a given sum of money, and assuming that during the duration of the contract 'Amr said, without any lawful grounds, I want to terminate that contract, could Zaid compel 'Amr to remain in his service until the expiry of the duration of their agreement? Yes, he could.'

I shall advise Abu Kasim of the existence of that *fatwa*, so as to put an end to a useless attempt.

There is no power but with God.
Qur'an, s. XVIII, 39

. . . NO DHIMMI of any standing in Beirut would leave himself without the protection of one or other of the consulates. Generally speaking the Greek Orthodox, who predominate here among the *dhimmis*, find protection with the Russian, Greek or British consulates; the Jews with the British; the Maronites with the French; and the Greek Catholics with the Austrian or the French.

Those *dhimmis* have made themselves indispensable to Western trade. They act as agents and intermediaries for foreign interests. They have the advantage of knowing the rudiments of foreign languages, mainly Italian and French, which they have acquired from the education they have received at one or other of the numerous missions' schools. Some of them have travelled and even resided abroad for a time. Despite the wordly advantages which can be reaped from foreign contracts, I do not believe that we should allow the minds of our youth to be meddled with by yielding to the adulteration of our traditional culture and the debasing of our saintly education. One day our great Sultan will shake off all the infidels' imports and we will return to our original state of purity. Gloomy days will not last for ever. Eventually only right shall prevail.

Protected *dhimmis* enjoy the same privileges and exemptions granted to the Europeans by our Master. They do not pay taxes and they are not submitted to our jurisdiction. Instead they account to consular tribunals.

Needless to say, they take full advantage of their position; they even try to make much of it, whenever possible. We at the *majlis* have lately examined the curious – I would say insolent – case of a *dhimmi* who at one time considers himself protected and at another time claims to be an Ottoman subject, following the needs of the moment. I believe that the case is worth a narration in some detail.

Khawaja (Mr, a title especially reserved for Christians) Nicolas Mitri has enjoyed Russian protection for the past ten years. He imports printed cotton fabrics from England and, from France, pearls, fine handkerchiefs, buttons and other luxury items. He also imports an increasing number of fezes from Austria. Fezes, *stamboulines* (frock-coats) and trousers are more and more in demand, especially among the civil servants and the *khawajat*.

This *dhimmi* is sued by his British supplier, for he refuses to pay in full the price of a consignment he had allegedly received after considerable delay. To avoid appearing before a consular tribunal formed of Russian and British judges, *Khawaja* Mitri has abandoned his consular protection and claims to be an Ottoman subject. His aim is to bring himself under the jurisdiction of Turkish judges, whose court will be attended by the British Consul as a simple observer. I cannot blame *Khawaja* Mitri for wanting to be answerable to his natural judges, but neither can I condone his antics. In any event, it was lucky that I did not have to decide on my own which courts will be competent to hear the case brought against him.

Khawaja Mitri arrived at the *majlis* dressed in local garments. I hardly recognized him, being accustomed to seeing him dressed like a European. We heard his plea and gave him leave. Then Mr Saba entered and delivered a speech which I have summed up for its mastery.

'When the British supplier agreed to deal with *Khawaja* Nicolas Mitri, it was with the implied understanding that in case of a dispute between them, that dispute would be settled by a consular tribunal.

'Now that a dispute has occurred – and I will not say here and now that *Khawaja* Mitri is the guilty party – he has none the less reneged on the implied agreement, which at the time had induced the foreign supplier to agree to deal with him in preference to tens of other merchants who would have been extremely happy to be in his stead.

'In all the *sharia* treatises it is stated that a case ought to be adjudicated after taking into consideration the circumstances which prevailed at the time that case developed. One party should not be permitted to change those circumstances to make them coincide with self-seeking interests.

'We will never allow that the spirit and contents of the Capitulations be swept aside to satisfy one man.

'Moreover, I beg you to tell *Khawaja* Mitri that if he persists in his resistance to being tried by the consular court – which was his choice when he acquired protected status – he will be boycotted by all Europeans. He would not be able to conduct a single transaction with any foreign party.'

The Pasha summoned *Khawaja* Mitri before the *majlis* and told him in detail what he should expect unless he abandoned the position he had foolishly taken.

Khawaja Mitri, not willing to lose face in a blatant manner, entrusted the settlement of the case to the Pasha's conciliation.

He, however, agreed to submit to the jurisdiction of the consular tribunal in the event that conciliation failed.

... IT IS BELIEVED that events of the same nature occur in series, three at a time generally speaking but not necessarily. Events involving a *dhimmi* were lately the city's lot. The latest of the series took place a few days after the *majlis* dealt with the case of *Khawaja* Nicolas Mitri and resolved it in the wisest fashion. Here we do not want any trouble with the Europeans and their protected, so long as everybody knows his station and does not overstep his limits. What we think of the non-believers should be kept in our hearts and not brought into the open. The time is not in favour of over-zealousness.

Apart from the latest near-catastrophe which involved the Austrian Jew, I cannot recall anything worth mentioning, whether during the Egyptians' time or after their departure. Then all of a sudden two incidents took place in succession as if someone was deliberately trying to stir up trouble in the city.

The first one occurred not long ago in the Souk al-Attareen (the perfume market). A woman who could be identified as a non-Muslim despite being veiled was passing there, riding an ass and accompanied by a servant. At one time she had to go by a coffee shop which is reputed to be the haunt of ruffians and false witnesses; all of them I know too well, for on occasion one or the other appears before me and swears to having been the witness to a given transaction, deed or incident which in fact he had never heard of or seen before the reward which "jogged his memory".

The moment that woman came in view of one of the ruffians who happened to be in the coffee shop, he sprang off his low stool, placed himself before the woman's mount and refused to allow it to proceed. At the same time he was hurling at her various insults for no reason at all.

Before long a crowd surrounded the protagonists of that ugly scene and those behind pushed ahead in order to see better. In the bustle someone unconsciously urged the ass forward. The ruffian felt challenged and drew a long knife and was about to slash the poor animal about the head.

Several honest men were passing by. They saw the incident and placed themselves between the attacker and the woman, ordering him to leave. They were too many for him to argue and they were very menacing. No man worthy of that appellation would have tolerated letting him get away with his unprovoked attack. Fortunately, many such men were at hand.

The other incident took place this morning and could have had more dire consequences but for the divine mercy. Near the Greek Orthodox Cathedral of Saint George I saw a band of young boys, the eldest no more than twelve, surrounding one individual who remained motionless, his head bent. Moments later I found out that he was the Greek Orthodox bishop. The villainous rascals were taunting the poor man, dancing round him to prevent his walking away from their naughtiness. One of the young devils even spat on him. I could not bear the sight of that and I interfered vigorously. My appearance and a few blows judiciously distributed did marvels. The boys disappeared.

I took the bishop by the hand and led him away from the place of his predicament. He could not find enough words to thank me.

. . . WHO CAN explain to me the meaning of the dream I had last night? If I seek the help of Umm Sobhiya, who is renowned for interpreting dreams and nightmares, she will most certainly give me a vaguely worded explanation so she will not be wrong whatever happens afterwards in real life. That dream is haunting me; I could not erase it from my mind whatever I did during the day.

I vividly remember myself floating in the air above the heads of a large group of people, all wearing grey and turning round endlessly. They paid no attention to me, being completely absorbed in their thoughts – probably as gloomy as their clothes and their faces. Suddenly, the crowd came to a standstill, then menacingly advanced towards the slender figure of a woman who appeared from nowhere. The woman was clad in white, except for the red slippers which emerged from beneath her long robe. That figure could only be Mrs Saba, and she needed my help. I extended my hand to deliver her from her tormentors, but she did not see me and nor was I able to reach her, despite several desperate attempts.

As suddenly as the mob threatened the innocent woman, it calmed down. People resumed going round for no obvious reason. The white form evaporated and disappeared as inexplicably as she had intruded.

At this point, I started falling down at great speed and was about to crash on the colourless crowd when I woke up and escaped the undesirable fate which was awaiting me. I should have felt relieved, but I was not. Reality is as grim as my dream. Grey is the colour of my entire life. Torpor and mediocrity reign supreme here and I cannot avoid them even in my dreams. After all, I need no one to unravel the meaning of my night vision; I live it every day.

. . . THE PASHA, the *Mufti* and several other *a'yan* (notables) all congratulated me on my timely intervention, which saved the Greek Orthodox bishop from the mob's hands. Everyone deplored the incident and thanked the Almighty for making me pass by when I was wanted as the humble instrument of His mercy.

It was during a *majlis* session mostly devoted to looking at the bishop's misfortune that I was fêted. Although the bishop did not want any more fuss about his ordeal, the Pasha had a different view. Pressed by the Russian consul, he wanted to know whether the assault on the bishop and the ugly episode in the Souk al-Attareen were planned. He ordered the police and his spies to conduct an inquiry into the two matters, then summoned us to hear the results of their investigation. We were told that most of the youths who importuned the bishop were Druzes, sons of refugees from the Mountains, and that their base deed was in all probability one of the consequences of the savage war which set their community against the Maronites a couple of years ago.

The ruffian who obstructed the woman's passage in the souk was caught by the police and found to be a confirmed drunkard. He was flogged a few lashes and warned to breach the peace no more.

When the *majlis*'s session ended and we were about to leave, the *Mufti* took me aside and alluded to a lawsuit pending in my court. He made me understand that the plaintiff was a relative of his and that he wanted me to know his connection with the case not – God forbid – to turn wrong into right, but for me to give the case all my attention and resolve it with diligence. I reassured the *Mufti* that I would do my best to satisfy him.

. . . THE CASE which raised the interest of the *Mufti* required a visit to the scene of the conflict. Bakr Kronfol complains that his neighbour, Sa'ad Bawwab, has two new windows which overlook his courtyard, where his *harem* walk, cook, sit and do hundreds of things a day. Kronfol complains further that his neighbour uses the terrace of his house, as do all Beirutis, except that his terrace has no parapet, making the view better and the offence graver.

I decided not to rely on any witnesses but to visit Bawwab's house myself. Hence with my clerk, the witnesses of the proceedings and the two litigants, we proceeded towards the premises which have prompted the dispute. We were followed by several loiterers, who probably thought we were about to unearth buried treasure.

Our destination was in Souk al-Cotton, not far from where *muallem* Shibli lives. I told myself it would be a good occasion, afterwards, to call on him and inquire about Khalid's studies.

At the bottom of his house the defendant clapped his hands to make our presence known to the women of the household, then we ascended the stone stairs which lead to the first floor, consisting of a *liwan* (an open room), three rooms each with an internal half-ceiling made of wood, a small kitchen and wooden stairs which take you to the roof. The *hareem* had obviously gathered in one of the rooms which was not to be inspected, because the house seemed uninhabited. In the two remaining rooms I saw for myself, and all the witnesses saw the same, that unquestionably the two windows overlooked Kronfol's courtyard. I was somehow relieved, because I would be able to oblige the *Mufti* with no harm done to justice.

I was sure that the view from the terrace would be likewise the view from the two windows, but I insisted on inspecting it for myself so no one could challenge the seriousness of my investigation.

I have a predilection for terraces, especially in the morning and the evening, as soon as the cold days are over. From the top of the house one can see the sun, 'smell the air', water one's pots of mint, parsley and flowers and watch the flight of the dozens of pigeons and sparrows which streak the sky. When anything out of the ordinary occurs in the streets below, the terraces are, practically speaking, the only prospect for a view, which is attained by leaning over the parapet.

Bawwab's terrace has no parapet and the view from there commands Kronfol's courtyard and even the interior of his house. I made it clear to Bawwab that he has to condemn his two new windows and erect a parapet on the terrace high enough to prevent any indiscretion.

Then I left our party and walked towards the end of the souk where *muallem* Shibli lives.

I shouted his name. He came down as quickly as he could and we strolled side by side towards the port. Abu Darwish's café seemed very inviting, so we entered and ordered drinks. Unwilling to question *muallem* Shibli about Khalid without a suitable exchange of civilities first, I enquired about his health. He enquired about mine, then I engaged in an approach which, I believed, would lead into the purpose of this meeting.

'*Muallem* Shibli,' I asked, 'is there any particular publication you have enjoyed lately? . . . What are the books that you recommend your advanced pupils to read?'

The answer came slowly, as if he was tormented by an incessant and insidious pain: 'Our literature is in a state of decadence . . . no, stagnation. Practically speaking, nothing new has been produced for years and years. Even our past masterpieces are hard to find in this barren place.

'We have in this country about a dozen printing presses; nearly every religious community, and each mission, owns one. Instead of making use of them for the benefit of education and progress, conflicting versions of the Scriptures are reproduced and put in the people's hands, adding to their confusion and bewilderment.

'The Biblists try to convert the Druzes, who in turn have cunningly requested from the Grand *Mufti* of Istanbul that he send his scholars to teach them the Islamic faith. The Maronite Patriarch threatens excommunication to any of his flock who dares communicate with non-Catholic Christians; the Greek Orthodox have taken him at his word and chosen to side with the Druzes during the latest distressing events. No wonder that barrenness is all that is found in such surroundings. We will never make this ground a fertile one unless we liberate ourselves from all the chains which shackle us.'

I did not understand why *muallem* Shibli was so much hurt by an endemic situation which is the inevitable fate of stray people, as he should have known. I felt that my question had diverted the conversation away from the object of my calling, but I could not immediately retreat from what I had myself started. So I asked, 'You are a man of letters and good sense, what do you recommend for a revival . . . I mean, a literary revival?'

Muallem Shibli's answer burst out, as if all his pain had disappeared: 'When, at the age of twelve, I finished learning to read and write, I told my father I wanted to be a priest. The truth is that I longed for more education and the possibility of travelling abroad.

'After a few years in a Greek Catholic convent, I was sent to the Vatican for further religious studies. Paris was too close and too radiant to be shunned, so I went there and learned the French language.

'Forgive me for such a long introduction. What I would like to tell you is that when in Paris I became familiar with a literary world I never dreamed could exist. Thoughts that, in the seminary, we did not allow even to cross our minds are expounded and developed in beautiful writings which convey bold ideas and concepts. I read whatever books I could find by the great French philosophers and writers Rousseau, Voltaire, Balzac and Hugo. After that I abandoned the idea of priesthood, to the profound distress of my family. I left my village in total disgrace and came to live here.

'To answer your question, I would say that the only way for us to improve and be productive is to translate those French books and learn from them.'

Despite my earlier wish to put an end to that conversation as soon as was proper, I decided to pursue it a little further, for I felt piqued by what I had heard.

'*Muallem* Shibli,' I objected, 'if we draw from foreign sources, what will happen to our own patrimony?'

The answer came with no hesitation: 'Our classical literary patrimony is prestigious, there is no doubt about that. We have in the past even transmitted to the Franks a Greek heritage they had once possessed and then lost, for the same reasons which are the direct cause of our state of decadence. It is only fair that at a time when we need assistance, from whatever quarter, we turn to the same Franks, who owe us so much.'

Unconvinced, I left our discussion at that stage and asked, 'What about Khalid? Are you satisfied with him? Is he making progress?'

Muallem Shibli hesitated a few seconds, then spoke as if he was relieved by my question: 'I am glad you asked, for I did not know how to open this subject with you. Khalid is a good boy, full of energy, but, frankly speaking, he is wasting his time and mine, and you are wasting your money. He is unable to concentrate long on his studies. I have tried to find out where his interest lies and I must say – nowhere, as far as learning is concerned. I am sorry I did not succeed in infusing Khalid with any interest in learning.'

I was listening to *muallem* Shibli with consternation and deep disappointment. I tried not to show my real feelings, however, and after a few minutes I left the café.

. . . THE MORE I relive my discussion with *muallem* Shibli, the more angry I get. The man is dangerous; he is capable of poisoning the minds of his pupils with his revolutionary ideas. At times ignorance can be bliss indeed.

No wonder Khalid is confused. His teacher is responsible for his disarray. I blame myself for having submitted Khalid to such an ordeal. I should not have relied on my first impression of this *muallem* Shibli; instead I should have had the discussion we were involved in at Abu Darwish's before I entrusted him with my son. What I have to do is find another teacher for him, and all will be well.

. . . AFTER A NIGHT of reflection I decided to seek the advice of Sheikh 'Abdel Rahman, my Sufi master and local head of the Qadiriyyah brotherhood (a famous Sufi order founded in the twelfth century AD).

It was Thursday and on this day every week, before the evening prayer, Sheikh 'Abdel Rahman holds a session of *dhikr* (repetitive invocation of God's name in ritual order) at the Zawiya al-Towba (the Prayer Room of Repentance).

I went there just when the master was about to start a *dhikr khafi*, which is performed quietly in a low voice. I was relieved, for I do not particularly enjoy the other *dhikr*, performed with processions, playing of music and other exuberant manifestations which I find rather embarrassing. We were about twenty and we all sat as at prayers, recited the *Fatiha* (the first chapter of the Qur'an) and repeated:

'God the Hearer
God the Seer
God the Knower.'

Then followed *dhikr* and meditation upon some verses of the Qur'an. There is one particular verse which I cherish, for it affirms the literal meaning of the Scripture and in addition opens the path for uncovering the hidden one:

> *He is the First and the Last, the Manifest and*
> *the Hidden, and He has full knowledge of all*
> *things.*

Qur'an, s. LVII, 3

When the ceremony ended and the evening prayer had been performed, I made Sheikh 'Abdel Rahman understand that I needed to speak to him in private. After the departure of the last of the faithful, I reported to him my discussion with *muallem* Shibli and expounded my worries about Khalid.

Sheikh 'Abdel Rahman was listening with great intensity. He did not interrupt me once but waited patiently until I had finished. He then said, looking at the wall behind me as if he were reading some inscription that he alone was able to see, 'Only one Book guides to the Truth and to a straight Path. Beyond that Path there is darkness and Hell. Owing to the Almighty's bounty you have realized the danger before it was too late. Praise be to God.'

'Sheikh 'Abdel Rahman,' I remarked, 'is it not the Prophet – peace be on him – who said, "Strive after learning even if you have to go as far as China"? I am convinced that we have to go along with progress, without, of course, losing any of our traditional legacy and most of all without having to heed any fallacy.

'I want Khalid to learn foreign languages. Unfortunately I have to choose between two evils: on the one hand, an unfrocked priest who seems to contrast religion with reason to the advantage of the latter, and on the other, missionaries and foreign priests who claim one's soul as a price for their tuition.'

Sheikh 'Abdel Rahman was quick to observe, 'I have not known a better man than you, O Abu Khalid. Why do you feel obliged to give your son an education unlike the one you have had? Do you believe that he can fare better in life if he knows more?'

I retorted, 'Khalid, it seems, will not be a scholar; let him at least be a rich merchant. One day I might be able to give him a modest capital to start with. The capital will not bear fruit unless he is better equipped than other merchants.

'Nowadays, business and trade are conducted in different ways than in the past. Foreign merchants with a scant knowledge of Arabic used to bring their goods to us and store them in the *khans* until sold to the inhabitants. Now you write and receive correspondence in foreign languages; you even travel to distant countries and outwit your competitors. If you hire a translator, he will gain access to your commercial affairs and, sooner than you expect, he will brush you aside and eliminate you.

'Why should Khalid not be like Gerios Antoun and better? What Gerios has is his knowledge of foreign languages and his contacts with the Franks.

'Tell me, where should I turn to secure for Khalid the same opportunities without subjecting his tender faculties to trying experiences?'

Sheikh 'Abdel Rahman is an outstanding spiritual man; he, however, had enough good sense to see my point. He reflected for some time and said, 'The Seal of the Prophets – peace be on him – was himself a merchant, and did not hesitate to deal with *dhimmis* whenever his trade required it.

'We are fallible and he was not, thus we should equip ourselves as best we can before engaging in deals outside the *umma* (the community of Muslims). If that means that foreign languages have to be learned, so be it.

'Between the two evils I advise you to leave Khalid in

muallem Shibli's care. At least Khalid's mind will not be poisoned by the teaching of another faith. Although religion and reason have coexisted from time immemorial, eventually and inevitably religion has triumphed, either owing to moments of human weakness or to instances of heavenly bliss.

'Even if *muallem* Shibli tries, in an oblique way, to disparage his religion, that will not affect ours.'

. . . THERE ARE brief moments during the afternoon when the world seems to be at a standstill. Amplified shadows seize large areas from brightness and nature pauses, balancing between day and night; sparrows silently cruise the sky, making themselves less conspicuous, and conversations from one terrace to another cease, all in a futile bid to delay the approach of darkness. But that cannot be, and moments later a black mantle enwraps the distant mountains, stained with purple streaks, and causes them to blend into obscurity; only their highest crests, crowned with snow, can still be seen, or, more probably, guessed. One by one, opulent lanterns and humble oil-lamps and tapers are lit, bringing comfort to the melancholic heart. Yet once the night is well in place, sadness disappears, because the prospect of the dismal phenomenon was more distressing than its actual occurrence, and because another glowing tomorrow can now be anticipated.

Whenever weather and time permit, I spend the last bright moments of the day on my roof terrace, and invariably experience identical ambivalent feelings, yet made less intense owing to the repetition of the same phenomenon which generates them. That is what I did this evening, with all the family sitting round me. When I bought this modest house, I made sure that the terrace would be well protected from the neighbours' watchful eyes and I had a suitably elevated parapet erected all around the roof.

In the midst of my own small world, surrounded by my beloved family, I felt contented and thanked the Almighty for His bounties. I also felt that the moment was appropriate to tell 'Aisha of my plans for her future, and on the same occasion to make Umm Khalid realize that her friendship with Umm Kasim must be restrained.

I spoke of my old friendship with Abu Kasim, of his wealth and of my joy when he told me that he had chosen 'Aisha to be his wife.

Umm Khalid was quick to react to the news. She said that she was certain that when 'Aisha was under Abu Kasim's *'usma*, she would be treated as if she were in her father's house. She then added, 'Umm Kasim is a dear friend and I am aware of all her virtues, but I also know how insufferable a wife she was. The mere fact that she lasted in Abu Kasim's house for so long is an ample indication of how good and kind this man is.

'Nevertheless, make sure, O Abu Khalid, that 'Aisha's *mahr* (dowry) will give her adequate security in case – God forbid – the bad eyes of the persons we know and do not know wreck the marriage. Abu Kasim is extremely wealthy, and to keep up with his standing he will willingly accept to undertake the payment of a large sum as a *muakkhar* (portion of the dowry made payable only on the termination of the marriage).

'Against the bad eyes I will give 'Aisha plenty of charms and amulets to hang around her neck and to suspend in her husband's home, yet the promise of a handsome amount of coins will not do any harm.'

I was pleased with Umm Khalid's commonsense and I made my feeling plain to her, saying, 'Woman, you are a good mother. The trousseau of your daughter will be taken to her husband's house by so many hands that it will be the subject of envious accounts for a long time. I have put aside a sum of money that we may spend on new garments and utensils for 'Aisha. I am also willing to provide her with one of the most expensive chests. If, however, you think that a red and green one made here, in Beirut, is not rich enough for your daughter, I will ask Gerios Antoun to buy a mother-of-pearl chest from Damascus.

'For sure, Abu Kasim will want a sumptuous *'urs*

(celebration) and *walimah* (feast). The Governor may even honour us with his presence. I believe this marriage, which will seal the alliance of our family with Abu Kasim's family, will further the social standing of both.

'Woman! Beware others' jealousy and remember that envy was explicitly mentioned among the forces which are endowed with a sort of evil, and remember what the Almighty enjoined us to say:

> *". . . I seek refuge with the Lord of the Dawn . . . from the mischief of the envious when he envieth."*
>
> Qur'an, s. CXIII, 1, 5

'Do not mention the planned marriage in front of anyone until we draw up the *kitab* (contract of marriage). Soon I will send two witnesses who recognize 'Aisha's voice for them to give evidence that they have heard her constituting me as her *wakil* (mandatary) to contract marriage on her behalf.'

When I finished my recommendations to Umm Khalid, I suddenly realized that I had neglected to give any attention to 'Aisha, whom I expected to see utterly thrilled with joyful excitement. I looked at her and saw her motionless, her face white as a shroud. My worries for her health immediately resurfaced and brushed aside pleasant thoughts and future plans. I must summon Dr Caporelli at once to examine her and cure her. Otherwise what kind of bride will 'Aisha be in her present state?

JUMADA AL-AKHIRAT 1259 (June 1843)

*A case of apostasy; the British Consulate woos the
Jesuits; a new commercial venture; the case of the
abducted little girl; the Qadi and the fortune-teller . . .*

. . . HE WAS YOUNG and foolish. He thought that the only
obstacle to his marriage with the beautiful Nafisa was his
religion, so he embraced Islam, went to her father and made
plain his intention to wed her. Hanna was a penniless
Armenian, and his proposal was turned down by Nafisa's
father with little ceremony and a few words of advice,
including the well-known proverb: 'Stretch your legs
according to the length of your quilt.'

A few years later the young fellow, who called himself by
now Yehya and had amassed a small fortune peddling goods
among the Bedouins, fell in love once more, but this time it
was with a girl who belonged to his former religion. The girl's
father banned him from her sight. It was obvious that Yehya's
rebuff was due to his conversion to the true religion. Yehya's
second misfortune of the heart took place during the Eygptian
occupation. He presumptuously felt safe enough to revert to
the religion of his fathers; therefore he renounced Islam,
readopted his former name and married the Armenian girl he
loved.

During the same period of time Yehya, or Hanna,
quarrelled with one of his occasional business partners and the
dispute degenerated into a lasting bitter hostility.

After the Eygptians' withdrawal, the case of Yehya was
reported to the Governor. The accusation directed against him

was one of apostasy, punishable by death. For months the Governor took no action. I was myself aware of Yehya's whole story but I felt that the Governor knew best what to do and what not to do. Furthermore, if I am not asked, I do not interfere with the policy of those in control.

The Governor's idleness was not to the liking of the hardliners among the members of the *majlis*. Headed by Abu Ibrahim, they made their voice heard and eventually the Governor was compelled to submit Yehya's case to the *majlis*.

The consuls of the European powers all went into frenzied action to prevent the execution of the apostate, who had by that time been thrown into gaol. Colonel Rose went to the Governor asking for Yehya's release; the French Consul lobbied the *Mufti* for the same purpose; and Mr Saba came to seek my advice about this unfortunate matter.

This is what I told the dragoman: 'You had better leave Yehya in gaol for his own safety. That man has lost the protection of the law by his act of apostasy. If he is released and he is killed, the killing would be morally wrong, for the apostate was not given the chance to re-embrace the Faith, but the executioner would incur no penalty of the law.'

My advice obviously raised Mr Saba's interest. That man, who came to me extremely disquieted, now had a glimmer of expectation in his eyes. He inquired, 'You have mentioned, O Abu Khalid, a chance to be given to the apostate. Do you mean by that, that before sentence is passed on him he should be given the possibility of going back to Islam?'

'Yes,' I replied. 'According to Abu Hanifa's teaching, he should be given that option for three days and if he entertains any doubts or irresolution, efforts must be made to remove them by presenting him with irrefutable evidence about the truth, and offering him all the clarification and teaching that he may need.'

A jubilant Mr Saba thanked me and departed.

A few days later I was glad to hear that Yehya had taken

advantage of the option offered to him. He had repented, uttered the *shehada* and reverted to Islam.

Everyone, except Abu Ibrahim and his clique of chauvinists and sufferers from cheap European imports, rejoiced at the happy ending brought to a troublesome affair. Apparently they had heard of the appeasing role I had played and of the advice I had given in compliance with the main teaching of the *sharia*. Reason and compassion were not what they wanted to see prevailing. They were intent on trouble and confrontation. From now on I have to be careful, for I have made for myself powerful enemies.

> *But God has full knowledge of your enemies;*
> *God is enough for a Protector; and God is*
> *enough for a Helper.*
>
> Qur'an, s. IV, 45

. . . I TOOK Mr Saba to my roof terrace and dismissed the boy after he had served us sherbet and lit our pipes. Tobacco's aroma and an afternoon sea breeze combined to make us elated for a moment, then the dragoman took the initiative of the conversation with the following words.

'We are deeply grateful to you, O Abu Khalid. The case of the foolish Armenian could have ended in violent death with alarming consequences. You, with compassion and wisdom, have taught us the way of avoiding the spilling of blood and have removed the prospect of a strained relationship with Her Majesty's Government.

'We are sincerely thankful and deeply indebted to you. That friendship of ours will remain for ever. As a token of our deep esteem, I beg you to accept this watch, made by the finest craftsman in London.'

Mr Saba placed at my feet a most beautiful gold watch, as well as a purse made of fine leather, then proceeded: 'I heard that soon you will be giving your elder daughter in marriage and I thought that a gift of gold coins would be appropriate and would allow you to choose for yourself what is best for her. I implore you not to turn down my request for your assistance with this matter.'

I was taken aback by the sumptuous gift and I realized how refined a man of the world the dragoman was, for he had placed the watch and the purse on the floor and did not hand them over to me. That means that if the need arises, I could always swear that I did not take them from him or from anybody else. What I did was to pick them up from the floor. Furthermore, that gift was not a condition for the assistance I had extended, it came after the event and as a sign of friendship, thus I felt completely free to take it.

Obviously the dragoman had unfinished business with me, for he accepted my offer of coffee and a new pipe, which were instantly brought. After a short pause – just the kind of silence which could only be enjoyed by two old friends – Mr Saba opened a new subject in these carefully chosen terms.

'My Government's policy in the Provinces is an open book, unlike the intrigues of some other European representatives. What we want to achieve is a lasting peace among the religious communities of the Mountains under the enlightened rule of His Majesty the Sultan. We want to help all of them with no exception and assist them to repair or replace the properties destroyed during the war and to start new projects, in particular new schools.

'Our good intentions are questioned by other governments which seek to divide in order to rule, and which, for that purpose, bestow their protection on one community at the exclusion of the others.

'Faithful to its line of action, my Government has extended a helping hand to the Jesuits, those Catholic priests who are at best ignored by the French Consul, when they are not victimized by him. It is not that the Consul has a personal grudge against them, or any animosity towards them; it is because the French government does not see their Order as a docile instrument of its foreign policy. The Order includes priests who belong to a variety of nations. Some of them were even at war with France some time or other. No wonder the French distrust it. We have offered to pay for the establishment of a Catholic Anglo-Maltese college in Mount Lebanon. A suitable residence is available at Ghazir in Mount Lebanon, only some five hours' walk from Beirut.

'Colonel Rose expects a positive answer from the Jesuits, who promised to write to their superiors asking their permission to go ahead with the project. I would like myself to hasten the process and, for that purpose, I need your help.'

I interjected: 'If you believe that a word from me will bring the Jesuits into your lap, that can mean only that you have a much higher opinion of your helpless friend than he really deserves. Just tell me, how can I perform that miracle without the help of an obliging genie?'

My interlocutor smiled and said, 'There are other ways, oblique perhaps, but nevertheless very effective. What you would do within the *majlis* is to ask for the closure of the Jesuits' residence in Beirut because it was bought and enlarged without a *firman*. I am aware that the matter was brought to the attention of the *majlis*, which, however, did not take action. You can always reactivate the case, and I have no doubt in my mind that Abu Ibrahim and his clique will join in your request. They will make enough noise to allow you to make a strategic withdrawal behind their vociferous group.

'Their residence closed, the Jesuits will look for another location, which has to be in Mount Lebanon, where a *firman* is not needed. They, however, do not have the money to start a new establishment, and the French Government will not provide it for them, for its assistance is all pledged to another religious order, the Lazarists. With no other option left, the Jesuits will be most appreciative of our offer.'

I was pleased with the ingenious plan, which will allow me to be of more assistance to a grateful friend.

. . . I REMITTED the gold coins to Gerios Antoun for him to trade

89

for our mutual account. Gerios was reluctant to buy and sell any goods at this particular time, for the reason that currencies' values have not yet stabilized since the last devaluation. His advice was to buy in advance the crop of leaves of one or two mulberry plantations.

'The farmers,' he said, 'are always short of money and I can get coming crops for a very cheap price whenever the farmers see coins in hand.'

I explained to my agent-manager that the *sharia* forbids the sale of fruits or agricultural products which are non-existent. Even when they are in existence, sale is only permitted when they are no longer at the flowering stage but have attained their final appearance. The reason for that is to make sure that the object of the sale is not only present but also free from defect.

'The objective of the *sharia*,' I said, 'is to prevent exploitation of the weak by the strong and to protect human beings from their own folly and extravagance. Thus the *sharia* prohibits transactions where the price or the subject-matter is uncertain or unknown, and in general whenever a transaction entails a strong element of *gharar* (uncertainty, risk, speculation).'

I sensed it was a timely occasion to tell Gerios what he could and could not do with my money, hence I proceeded: 'Lending money for interest is also out of the question. *Riba* is prohibited by the Qur'an and the *Sunna* (deeds, utterances and tacit approvals of the Prophet). The offender will be the Companion of the Fire and will abide therein for ever.'

'Then what is it that I am allowed to do? How can I make your money bear fruit?' asked Gerios.

I replied, 'There are means, perfectly legitimate, which can alleviate the burden of the two prohibitions of *riba* and *gharar*. What one can do is to buy a given property or goods – provided they are in existence – for, let us say, 100 piastres, and resell the same subject-matter to the vendor for the price of 110 piastres, to be paid at a given time in the future. The transaction is not deemed a loan but a legitimate credit sale.'

I added a word of advice: 'One has also to make sure that the buyer for 110 piastres will be able to pay that amount when it becomes due; for that purpose it is always advisable to get the benefit of a pledge which secures payment.'

After that I left the money with Gerios, knowing that he would endeavour to fructify it without violating the law.

. . . NO JOY IS COMPARABLE to the divine delight felt by parents who recover their child, missing for twelve years and presumed dead. I had the privilege of being instrumental in reuniting a young woman with her natural family as a result of one of the most amazing cases ever brought to my court.

The case is worthy of the stories of *The Thousand and One Nights* and leaves no doubt in the mind that real facts are sometimes harder to believe than fiction.

The climax of the case occurred earlier this morning, when all the protagonists and a few others crowded into my small courtroom in the presence of the *Mufti* and other *'Ulema* (learned men) invited to join in examing the case. But I had better first narrate all the facts which were progressively revealed over the past months and found a happy conclusion on this very day.

Khalil Antoun is Gerios's uncle. The two men are very close to each other. In the wake of the Eygptian occupation Khalil, with his wife Samiha and their only child, Zahra, a girl of six, left their village in the Metn district and came to live in Beirut. Khalil had spent a few years in Alexandria and his acquaintance with Egypt's habits and customs made him believe that he could start a profitable business by providing the Eygptian army with what it needed and he could procure.

Houses located within the city's walls – or what remained of them – were at a price Khalil could not afford, so he bought a small house on the outskirts and settled there, joyful at being closer to Gerios's place and making good money out of his new business. Happiness was short-lived, for one afternoon Zahra disappeared from the small garden adjoining the house of her parents, where she had been playing on her own. She could be found nowhere.

Her father went to Gerios and informed him of Zahra's disappearance. Gerios proceeded forthwith to the Governor and begged for his help. The Governor, who is the father of a girl of the same age as Zahra, was moved to the extreme by Gerios's account; he gave an order to start searching for Zahra everywhere. He even sent town-criers, who shouted the little girl's name all around Beirut, Sayda and Tripoli, and invited anyone who knew anything about her to come forward.

All efforts were of no avail; the girl had disappeared as if the earth had swallowed her. Samiha, her mother, was heart-broken; her health deteriorated and she ended up spending more time on her sickbed than on her feet. Doctors and healers, from the town and from afar, called on her in turn.

Lately, Dr Caporelli was requested to examine her. He scrutinized Samiha for several minutes, then asked, in his fluent Arabic, 'O wife of Khalil, do you have a daughter who lives in Tripoli?'

The moment she heard that question, Samiha collapsed and burst into tears, unable to speak, but her eyes spoke for her; the fingers of her two hands were interlaced in silent prayer and her face was by now brightened by a hope she did not dare let out. Khalil told the doctor that their only daughter had disappeared twelve years ago, never to return. If she were alive she would be by now eighteen years of age. Khalil begged the doctor to tell them everything he knew about that girl in Tripoli.

The following is Dr Caporelli's account.

'A family by the name of Akrouni invited me to proceed to Tripoli to see a young girl who was complaining of stomach cramps. I did what I was requested to do and examined a girl, who was probably in her eighteenth year. When I examined *sitt* (Mrs) Samiha, I was amazed to find out that the girl's features and build are exactly as those of *sitt* Samiha.

'The girl told me in confidence that she was a Christian from Beirut and that she longed to be reunited with her parents. Now, with the story I heard from you and the story I have heard from her, and especially from her appearance, I believe there is a strong probability that the girl is your long-lost daughter.'

Khalil carefully took note of all the information he could get from Dr Caporelli, about the girl and where exactly the Akrouni family resides. He took all these facts to Gerios, who conveyed them to the Governor and to me.

The Pasha decided to proceed very discreetly before making a move. He instructed a lady from Tripoli, who was on his payroll, to befriend the Akrouni family, gather all the intelligence she could and report to him. In less than two months she was able to give the Pasha the following account.

'The girl, when she was six or seven, was snatched by a Bedouin and was sold to the Akrounis. She was given Khadra as a name and was first treated as a servant. When she grew up into a beautiful adolescent, they betrothed her to their son.

'The girl vividly remembers that her parents are Christians, and live in a house surrounded by mulberry trees and flanked by two palm trees. She also recalls a well in the proximity of the house. The Akrounis threatened to kill her if she ever considered going back to her natural parents.'

The Governor took the bold decision to bring the girl under guard to Beirut, for her own safety, and to submit her strange case to my court.

This morning the girl made her appearance before me and before the learned persons I have summoned to assist me in reaching a just decision in a most delicate problem.

Khalil, Samiha, Gerios and a few of their friends were there. Also present were the Akrounis, who had made the journey from Tripoli. As a precaution they were kept at a safe distance from Khadra – or was it Zahra?

The dragoman of the Consulate of France was also among us, and I had no doubt in my mind that he had already lobbied the *Mufti* on behalf of the Antouns.

At first the girl said she had no father and no mother. I ordered her to unveil her face. All those in attendance burst out, 'She looks exactly like her mother!'

Samiha, in tears, spoke to her in the following terms: 'Oh, Zahra, have you forgotten our love and devotion to you, have you forgotten your father and how much he spoiled you? Have you forgotten your uncle Nassim and your aunt Zeinab?'

The girl was apparently unmoved. Samiha pressed on: 'Zahra, my little girl, do you remember the well near our house? One day you tripped and fell into it – here is Gerios your cousin who saved your life. You are my girl, my girl, do you wish to kill me for the second time?'

At this juncture the girl awoke from her torpor and shouted, 'Mother, Mother!' and threw herself in Samiha's arms.

We all wept and it took us but a few minutes of deliberation before we decided that Zahra should be reunited with her natural parents.

O God, do not deny me any of my children. Do not let me see the demise or disappearance of any of them, but let me enter your Garden before any of them.

. . . NOT LONG after the dramatic episode which found a gratifying conclusion with the reunion of Khalil Antoun's family, Gerios came to me in order to make up his accounts regarding our past ventures. Although the time was during the afternoon and the sun had started its descent on the horizon, it was too hot to remain within the city walls, even on a roof terrace.

We decided to take a stroll in the direction of Minet al-Hussein bay. Our objective was a small café by the sea. Nothing comparable to Abu Darwish's stylish establishment, still it is comfortable and the scenery around it has a soothing effect. Mount Lebanon is well in the background and therefore appears less majestic and less threatening. The atmosphere which emanates from the place is one of serenity and peace, especially when the sea is unagitated, as it was when we arrived there.

Gerios showed me the accounts and calculated my share of the profits, which was far in excess of what I expected. He handed over to me a purse full of gold coins and thanked me, once more, for having allowed Khalil and Samiha to be reunited with the daughter they thought they had lost for ever. He mentioned his community's deep gratitude and admiration for my sense of justice and my fortitude. I was delighted by his gratifying words and by the handsome purse which I felt close to my bosom.

While we were both looking in silence at the sun getting ready to plunge into the waters with relief, a young gypsy girl came straight to me and with great boldness said, 'From your face, Master, I can see that you are a man of letters, very discerning and good-hearted.

'Let me see the palm of your hand and I will tell you not only what you are but also what to anticipate from the future.

'You are an extremely interesting subject, therefore I do not expect any fee from you, unless you decide out of your own good heart to give me a small reward.'

I was amused by the impudence of the girl, and impressed by her glib tongue. I admired her slender figure and delicate features. She somehow reminded me of 'Aisha, although the gypsy's complexion was much darker than that of my dear daughter.

Laughing, I extended my left hand, which she took gently and started scrutinizing my palm. As she traced the lines with her finger her whole demeanour changed. Her face became sombre and she looked at me with horrified eyes. She dropped my hand as if she were being burned and swiftly turned away, mumbling, 'Nothing, I see nothing . . . but blood, blood.'

Then she ran – as if there were a thousand devils on her heels. Gerios was quickly on his feet, trying in vain to catch the girl, to find out why she had behaved in such a way.

I watched with bewilderment and an inexplicable fear crept into my heart.

RAJAB 1259 (July 1843)

*Abu Kasim buys a new house; Abu Ibrahim's nephew
is sued before the Qadi; 'Aisha prepares her
trousseau; warning and requests from the dragoman;
'Aisha disappears . . .*

. . . I ACCOMPANIED Abu Kasim to look at a house he intends to
buy and live in once he marries 'Aisha. The house in question is
conveniently located, for it is adjacent to his present dwelling,
and the idea is that Abu Kasim's sons will continue to occupy
their quarters, whereas the existing reception area will be
joined to the latest acquisition to form the new couple's
habitation.

I immediately realized that the house coveted by Abu Kasim
shares the ownership of a private footpath with a neighbouring
house. That means that the two co-owners of the footpath
have a right of *shuf'a* (pre-emption) over each other's houses in
case of a sale to a third party. Provided he reimburses the exact
sale price, the footpath's co-owner, who retains possession of
his house, will acquire by preference the other house which is
the subject of the sale.

Abu Kasim was disappointed but I heartened him by telling
him that a simple legal device well tested in court, would
discourage the co-owner from the exercise of the right of
pre-emption. My advice was to split the sale into two
transactions; the object of the first one would be a single share
out of all the shares which stand for the house. The price of
that single share would be stated as very high; it would in fact
represent the major part of the agreed price for the whole

house. In a concomitant transaction the remaining shares would be sold for the balance of the price. Indeed the right of pre-emption exists with regard to the first sale, but the co-owner of the footpath would not want to exercise it, for that single share at such a high price would be of no avail to him.

Abu Kasim remarked, 'Surely, with your device, the right of pre-emption would also exist with regard to the second transaction and before long the co-owner of the path would be in possession of all the shares representing the house I want for myself.'

'Fortunately not,' I said. 'The pre-emption would be yours, due to the one share owned at the same time the remaining shares were acquired. As a joint-owner of that one share, you would be entitled to exercise the *shuf'a* by priority, because your right precedes your neighbour's right.'

'What if that neighbour asks me to take the oath that the two transactions are not a stratagem devised to defeat his right of pre-emption?' asked Abu Kasim.

I replied, 'Oath would not be granted, for the allegation, even if true, would not have any adverse legal consequence. The two transactions would be perfectly legal; what is in the minds of the parties has no bearing whatsoever on the validity of the acts they have contracted.'

Abu Kasim was obviously pleased; I was full of anticipation. With his money and my knowledge of the arcana of the law, we could do great things together.

. . . ABU KASIM'S youngest sister was married to 'Uthman, Abu Ibrahim's nephew, who repudiated her two years after the marriage. The girl had been raised and utterly spoiled by Abu Kasim, who took care of her after their father and mother died, when she was still very young. That is a fact, but 'Uthman is himself a good-for-nothing lad. He spends his time with his young friends, racing horses and throwing javelins on the outskirts of the pine forest.

Wickedly, 'Uthman refuses to pay to his divorced wife her

alimony and the *muakkhar* to which she is entitled. A number of mutual friends intervened in order to settle this unpleasant matter outside court, but the stubborn 'Uthman refused to listen to reason, although it is well known that he is solvent.

Abu Ibrahim's offer to pay in his stead was turned down by Abu Kasim, who proudly declared that his sister wants from her ex-husband what is rightly hers, not charity from anyone else. Eventually, and to my deep annoyance, the case was brought to my court. On the one hand, I am willing to satisfy Abu Kasim, especially because his sister is within her rights, but on the other hand, it is dangerous to alienate the powerful Abu Ibrahim.

What I will do is to temporize as long as possible. Who knows, maybe in the meantime an arrangement could be found and I would not be pressurized to take action.

If, after a waiting period, which I will stretch out for as long as possible, nothing happens, then I will caution 'Uthman to pay or to be incarcerated until he settles his debts.

I sincerely hope that I will be spared the hardship that this course of action will necessarily generate.

. . . 'AISHA AND HER SISTER are the daily visitors to Mariam's workshop. Sometimes Umm Khalid escorts them, but often she is too busy with her cooking and cleaning and sends Khalid or our young servant to accompany the two girls. The entire energy of the women of my house is focused on 'Aisha's trousseau. The smallest detail of a new garment is scrutinized and, if it is not to the liking of any one of the examiners, is brought back to Mariam. The poor girl must be fed up with all the fuss and the endless alterations requested of her. I have to remind the women that my purse is not filled up by a benevolent genie; they should go easy on unnecessary expenses. On the other hand, my future son-in-law is not just anybody; he is rich and successful. We have known each other since childhood and in no way must I lose face in my dealings with him. Moreover, he had better know how much I love my daughter and that no cost will be spared for her happiness. After all, she is the daughter of a man also eminent in his community, literate and well read. Others may have more money, but education and position are not to be scorned.

'Aisha herself can read the Qur'an. How many women in the city can pride themselves on the same? Probably no more than two or three. It can only be for the best to remind Abu Kasim that 'Aisha is treated like a queen in her father's house; that can entice him to treat her likewise when she is brought under his *'usma*.

And yet it is not every day that the representative of the great Queen will show me his gratitude, nor every day that my agent-manager will surprise me with profits much larger than anything I expected, 'Keep your white piastre for a black day'; surely that proverb, which represents one of the multiple aspects of the wisdom of our fathers, deserves to be heeded.

My late father – God have mercy on his soul – used to repeat for my benefit: 'Do not allow yourself to be in a situation where you need the assistance of anyone; people are your friends so long as you are not a burden to them.' How right he was. I have seen rich people and people in high office who, while prosperous or powerful, could not count the friends and courtiers surrounding them, and who found themselves alone and forsaken the moment their wealth or influence eluded them. As far as I am concerned, I do not have any illusions about the marks of respect shown to me. These marks are extended either out of fear or as a prelude to a request for some favour.

The moment I am no more a judge, my popularity will gradually dwindle and then my name will sink into oblivion, or, worse, people who showed me exaggerated respect in the past might wish to exact a petty vengeance for their earlier abasement and treat me with contempt. That is, unless I leave office rich enough to continue to command respect.

... MR SABA had expressed the wish to see me, first in private,

99

then in the company of Abu 'Abbas. He gave me the choice of the meeting place, and the dragoman's residence seemed to me quite appropriate. Thus I made arrangements to the effect that I would be there in the early part of the afternoon and that Abu 'Abbas would join us an hour later.

Looking deep into my heart, I must admit that the prospect of seeing the beautiful Mrs Saba gracefully moving about her luxurious surroundings assisted me in my decision. When I started this diary, I promised to be honest, at least with myself, and that promise I intend to keep. Often Mrs Saba's image haunts me at night; I would certainly not miss another chance of seeing her in the flesh. That was the other reason for the arrangement.

I was introduced by a black slave into the courtyard, where I was met by Mr Saba, who warmly greeted me and invited me to sit under the fruit and citrus trees, which provided protection against the heat of the sun. More freshness was contributed by the water running from a beautiful fountain located in the middle of the patio. Water was flowing from the mouths of two dolphins carved in white marble into the fountain's receptacle and from there into an open conduit which meanders around. The fountain was made of various coloured marbles which looked bright and shiny as they were constantly washed by the running water.

The image of paradise cannot be complete without a houri. Well, here she appeared after a short while. Mrs Saba brought us sherbets and other refreshments. To tell the truth, I do not remember what exactly she offered me, nor what I took; I had no eyes except for her. She was wearing a beautiful long shirt made of silk with yellow, white and blue stripes; the shirt generously exposed her bosom. Over this she had an open dress which invited you to imagine her magnificent shape; her hair was hidden under a scarf ornamented with several pieces of gold.

I looked at her feet, expecting to see her – or rather my – red slippers, but to my disappointment she came out of the house barefooted and slipped into a pair of *kubkab* (clogs), made of wood and inlaid with mother-of-pearl, which she probably found more suitable for an outdoor activity.

After she had civilly enquired about my health, she asked about Umm Khalid's well-being.

'*Ajallek* (apology to you), the woman is fine,' I replied.

Having displayed all the marks of a warm hospitality, Mrs Saba retired and left us to more serious business.

The dragoman silently puffed smoke drawn from a magnificent *narghile*, repeating the operation several times before he addressed me in the following manner.

'It is good to be among friends and I dare, O Abu Khalid, to consider myself your subservient and much obliged friend.'

I made a gesture of protest, but before I could say anything Mr Saba continued: 'Confidence is the necessary ingredient of a genuine friendship and, since our relationship can pride itself on that attribute, I can open my heart to you.

'The situation in the Lebanese Mountains is precarious. The division of the Mountains into two districts, one for the Druzes and one for the Christians, was carried out on a geographical basis, which means that the few Druzes who inhabit the Christian sector will be subject to Christian jurisdiction and the Christians who live among the Druzes will be subject to the latter's jurisdiction.

'That orderly system is rejected by the Maronites, who hold that the Christians in the Druze district are numerous and would suffer a great deal if they were not judged by Qadis and lords of their own community. Hence we suspect that the Maronites will bring their lawsuits to the courts of the coastal towns in order to avert Druze jurisdiction.

'My Government believes that if the Maronites are left with the freedom to choose a jurisdiction other than the natural one, that would undermine the authority of the Druze lords and judges, and, as a consequence, that would put into jeopardy the order wanted by the Sublime Porte for the Mountains. Abu

Khalid, it is in your power to contribute to the stability of this part of the Empire.'

'What is it I can do, with the modest means in my possession?' I questioned.

'A lot,' he replied. 'Chiefly what you can do is to send back to their natural judges any litigants from the Mountains who solicit the jurisdiction of your court. You can also encourage other Qadis to do the same.'

I nodded my acquiescence and resumed puffing smoke from my own *narghile*.

Moments later Abu 'Abbas made his entrance and joined us. Refreshments were brought to him by a slave, not by Mrs Saba. Being a *'aqil*, Abu 'Abbas was spared the view of an unveiled woman unrelated to him, and was not offered tobacco or coffee, which he had denied to himself when he was promoted to his class.

The dragoman welcomed Abu 'Abbas with the usual greetings, then said, addressing his newly arrived guest, 'You will be pleased to know that all the Druze sheikhs who took refuge in Damascus at our Consul's there are back in their homes in the Mountains. Unfortunately, not all news is as good as that. Some European powers press for the disarmament of your community and for extorting from it large damages to be paid to the Christians. I advise you to resist any such demands. I do not believe that armed resistance will be necessary, but your community must show enough determination to indicate that it would not hesitate to resort to arms if necessary.'

Abu 'Abbas was listening with great attention. Contrary to the attitude he had shown during his first encounter with the dragoman, this time he did not express polite protests of his inability. He was fully aware that these were trying moments for his community and that time was of the essence, and not to be lost on feigned modesty.

Mr Saba went on: 'Ammunition from Damascus has been distributed among the Druze families. Do not believe for one moment that the Christians have remained idle. They are making themselves ready as well, and we have been told that the inhabitants of Deir al-Kamar have bought a large quantity of gunpowder.

'The situation is extremely serious. Nobody wants another war in the Mountains, but one has to be prepared in case war breaks out. If you need help, you must know that you have me as a friend ready to assist.'

A prolonged silence followed Mr Saba's warning. I knew that the situation in the Mountains was volatile; but to hear details confirming it, from the mouth of a man as informed as Mr Saba, made me realize that the danger was real and pending. Abu 'Abbas was also lost in deep reflection; when he emerged from his meditations, he hastily took leave of Mr Saba.

I left not long after him, utterly resolved to provide all the assistance I can muster in order to avoid new bloodshed among the people of the Mountains.

. . . BEFORE THE MUEZZIN'S call for the *salat al-fajr* I woke up, feeling a presence in the room. It was Umm Khalid, leaning over my mattress with fear and tears in her eyes; she was tearing at a handkerchief with both her hands, her face distorted by grief. The only words she uttered were, ''Aisha, 'Aisha . . . where is 'Aisha?'

The first idea which came to my mind was that Umm Khalid was making her usual fuss when she needed an object or a person she was unable to find immediately. I tried to calm her down, showing her my customary composure, but she did not look at me or listen to me, and continued to repeat in a lugubrious voice, over and over again, 'Where is 'Aisha?' Fear crept in my heart, but I revealed nothing of it.

'What do you mean, where is 'Aisha?' I asked harshly. 'She must be either in her room with Khadijah, in the courtyard or on the roof terrace. You have only to search properly before starting one of your dramas.'

For the first time in our entire married life, I felt anger in

Umm Khalid's voice when she interjected, 'Do you believe that I would dare wake you up for no valid reason? I have searched the whole house, and the courtyard. I climbed myself to the roof and went to our neighbours, whom I woke up. I could not find 'Aisha; nobody has seen her since yesterday afternoon.'

Without a word I left my mattress and looked for my daughter. Eventually I had to accept that Umm Khalid was telling the truth.

By then I was really alarmed; a calamity must have befallen 'Aisha. The story of Zahra, the little girl abducted by a Bedouin, flashed through my mind, and for a moment I feared that my beloved daughter might herself have been the victim of a kidnap, but I dismissed the idea as absurd. 'Aisha is a grown-up girl; if anybody had tried to make her do what she did not want to do, her shouts would have alerted the entire neighbourhood. For some silly misunderstanding at home, she must have slipped out of the house without my permission and gone to her favourite aunt, who lives in the village of Shuayfat. I asked Umm Khalid to assemble the entire household, while I performed my ablutions and the first prayer of the day.

Neither Khalid, Khadijah or the young servant was able to shed any light on 'Aisha's disappearance. I decided to go to Abu 'Abbas and ask for his help.

I had only to cross the street to see Abu 'Abbas, whom I found full of sympathy and understanding. I fully realized that my predicament must have revived in him the very sad memory of the disappearance of Zein, his grandson, and of the subsequent news of his tragic and puzzling death. Although I was sure that this was the case, Abu 'Abbas did not allow his emotion to be brought into the open. He calmed my fears and ordered his eldest son to saddle one of his horses and ride to Shuayfat in search of 'Aisha. At the same time, he directed his remaining sons to comb the city for any news or sighting of her.

Abu 'Abbas's calm and energetic directions alleviated my

torment. My ordeal was now shared, with someone generous lending effective support, and that made its burden less hefty.

I warmly thanked my compassionate neighbour and left to attend to urgent cases in my court. On the way I asked myself whether to tell Abu Kasim of 'Aisha's disappearance, but I decided to wait a little longer. The emissary sent to Shuayfat might bring back good news; 'Aisha might be found, or she might reappear with a simple explanation of her absence.

I disposed of my court work as quickly as I could and, without taking any food, I decided to wait for Abu 'Abbas's eldest son at the south gate of the city. I told Umm Khalid where to find me in case 'Aisha appeared in the meantime.

The gateway is vaulted and provided a cool shelter from the summer heat. I sat there and became the focus of attention for astonished passers-by who, for the most part, recognized me and greeted me. Even the professional letter-writer, who had made the gateway his place of work and was normally too much submerged to distinguish anything around him, looked at me with surprise. I pretended not to take any notice and remained absorbed in my thoughts.

When I heard the muezzin calling for *salat al-'asr*, I prayed for 'Aisha's safety as I never prayed before, and made the promise to slaughter three sheep if she were home this evening.

Alas! It was not to be. As soon as I saw our gallant horseman, I realized that he was the bearer of no news. 'Aisha had not been seen in Shuayfat.

What should I do? What should I tell Abu Kasim, and all the others? It was too painful to confront Umm Khalid with no news. She was in a terrible state. I could not bear the commotion and took refuge in my room with my diary as confidant.

I feel feverish. That is certainly due to the hours I have waited at the gateway with no food and no water. I cannot write any more; I cannot think any more . . . Will tomorrow be another day of sorrow, or will I awake from a terrible nightmare?

... The Pasha welcomed Abu Kasim warmly and greeted me rather curtly. It was not an appropriate time for me to take offence, and I pretended not to have noticed his discriminating reception. I told him about 'Aisha's disappearance and his whole demeanour instantly changed. He showed compassion and readiness to help. He summoned the Chief of Police and gave him strict instructions to investigate 'Aisha's disappearance, with priority over all other cases. I know the Chief of Police well; he has several times in the past brought to my court recalcitrant debtors and litigants unwilling to attend a hearing.

When we left the Governor's office, Abu Kasim took leave of me, for his shop was unmanned that day, and promised to join me around noon. The Chief of Police asked permission to accompany me home and start his investigation from there.

When we arrived at our destination, he made a strange request: he wanted to see each member of the household alone and in private. That was odd, and I reluctantly accepted that Khadijah and Umm Khalid be seen by him outside my presence. Now I sincerely regret that I ever gave him permission for that. Not because the good man betrayed my trust or behaved other than respectfully, but because he was able to unearth the truth.

I did not want to know that truth; I would have preferred to be told of my daughter's death. That would have been simpler, and no shame would have been brought on my head.

That was not to be, for after a cleverly conducted interrogation Khadijah admitted that her sister had eloped with a man, and that that man was 'Ali, Abu Kasim's coffee-boy and shop assistant.

I was stunned by the news, and I did not even realize that the Chief of Police had left to pursue his inquiry and try to find the two culprits.

When I awoke from my torpor, I brought together Khadijah, Umm Khalid and the young servant. I did not include Khalid, for the poor boy must have been frightened enough by the Chief of Police's questions and, anyhow, he is too young to know anything about this dreadful matter.

I started beating the young servant with a rod, until my arm began to hurt. The boy was yelling and shouting, and continued to yell and shout even after I stopped the beating. When I turned towards Khadijah, she was pale and shaking all over; with no need for further intimidation, she revealed everything she knew. This is the story of the ultimate treachery and perfidy as she told it.

'Abu Kasim's shop is where we often go to buy fabrics for our garments and for the household. Shortly after 'Aisha and 'Ali met there, they fell desperately in love with each other. I saw this happening; I tried to prevent it, but I could not. Whenever I attempted to stop 'Aisha from seeing 'Ali, she would become sick and refuse to take any food. I even threatened to expose her and tell you everything. She then fixed expressionless eyes on me and promised to kill herself if I did that. Her quiet countenance and seriousness left me in no doubt that she would carry out her threat.

'I did not want to be responsible for my sister's death. I now know that I have failed you . . . I beg you to forgive me.'

Khadijah went on her knees, pleading mercy. Umm Khalid was in tears and about to hit her. I stopped her, wanting to know the whole story before punishment was inflicted. I bombarded Khadijah with questions.

'Tell me who else knew about this outrage? Who helped them? How and where did they meet? Where are they now?'

Still on her knees, Khadijah said, 'They used to meet at the Jewish dressmaker Mariam's. She was the intermediary between them; she was the one who made their exchange of correspondence possible and offered her workshop as a meeting place. Do not be mad with me, but Khalid also took part in this cursed matter. Whenever he accompanied us to

107

Abu Kasim's shop – and we always went there after making sure that Abu Kasim was away – or to Mariam's, 'Ali used to buy sweets for Khalid and send him out to play with other boys in the street. He used to do the same with the servant when it was he who was with us.'

When I heard that Khalid was unwittingly used in such a base way I became furious and delivered a few strokes on Khadijah's shoulders. Umm Khalid joined me in the beating.

'Where are they now?' I suddenly asked, hoping to catch her by surprise.

She replied in a high-pitched voice, 'Believe me, I do not know. All I know is that yesterday before sunset they left town, separately, to meet an accomplice who would be waiting for them at the south gate with two mules. That is all I know.'

A pallid and broken Abu Kasim joined me soon after. The Chief of Police had told him the whole story. He kept mumbling, 'This is why he did not open the shop this morning . . . shame, shame on me . . . on us. How can I ever face friends and foes after what has happened?'

That was exactly the question that was torturing me . . .

SHA'BAN 1259 (August 1843)

The Qadi*'s lament; 'Ali and 'Aisha*
are located; a trip to Jabal 'Amil . . .

. . . It is the affected commiseration of my familiars and of those I barely know that I cannot stand. Lately how many times have I heard, repeated for my sake, proverbs the like of: 'My heart is for my child, but my child's heart is of stone . . .' and, 'Beware of the one to whom you have done a good turn . . .'?

My predicament has made me look vulnerable, and encouraged people remotely acquainted to approach me and bestow on me advice and counsel. The most foolish of men have taken heart from my trying situation and felt reassured about their own intellect and wisdom. I have had to suffer the ignominy of their patronizing approaches and pretend to be grateful.

What affected me most was Abu Kasim's attitude. He was hurt in his pride and could not accept rejection. He quite naturally put the blame on his shop assistant, repeating in front of his visitors, 'I anticipated something vile from this cheat, but nothing compared to this monstrous deed . . . What do you expect from a coffee-boy?' It occurred to none of those present to remind Abu Kasim of his own origins and of the source of his fortune. Fortune causes short memory but creates lengthy ancestral lines.

Believe it or not, Abu Kasim gave me the cold shoulder, as if it were not enough for me to suffer my daughter's treason; I have also to endure the tacit reproach of a friend

109

dear to my heart despite all the flaws in his character.

I promised myself not to show my dismay but to give him time for a fairer perception of this shameful matter. After all, I am much more the victim than he pretends to be. My daughter has betrayed me and eloped with a man who does not belong to our religious sect and who is below her social standing. Above all, my permission was not sought and anyhow would never have been granted if requested. Abu Kasim's disappointment is trifling in comparison to my shame.

Umm Khalid's first reaction was to shut herself up and refuse to see the women of the neighbourhood who came to her under the pretence of comforting her, but were in fact bored to death and eager to learn of any stimulating, piquant detail. I instructed Umm Khalid to pull herself together and receive those females well, lest the insult of not welcoming them should become another ground for their unkind gossip. From my quarters I could hear them speculating about the whereabouts of the unsanctified couple, laughing and speaking simultaneously. Coffee and *narghiles* were consumed all day long, adding material loss to the loss of face I have already sustained. Whatever the cost may be, I have to confront the situation, hoping that soon the commotion will die down. I will then be left with my sorrow, shared with Umm Khalid and nobody else. Although Khadijah is very affected by her sister's having run away, youthful insouciance will necessarily prevail and she will soon forget the whole episode. Khalid is too young to understand what happened or to store any bad memory in his tender mind.

At first I was inclined to blame Umm Khalid for her daughter's conduct, but I took pity on her when I witnessed her grief and saw fear in her eyes. I realized how much she dreaded my reaction. It was then that, for the first time in the eighteen years of our marital relationship, I took her two hands in mine, in a gesture of affection, and told her, 'Do not worry, I will bring back our daughter.'

... THE PROMISE I made to Umm Khalid was easy to say but hard to keep. Neither the Governor nor the Chief of Police was able to give me a clue as to where 'Aisha might be. I do not know what to do or where to turn. Maybe I should forget all about this ungrateful daughter of mine and consider her dead. That would have been the disposition of mind of most of the people I know, if faced with the same predicament; I, however, have different feelings. Something tells me that my daughter might be unhappy and regret her deed. Above all, there is Umm Khalid. Following the hasty promise I made to her, she looks to me as a champion and a saviour. I can see in her pleading eyes conflicting signs of despair and hope. I must find 'Aisha. I must know whether she is dead or alive and, if alive, whether she wants to come back home or stay with the husband she has chosen without my blessing. If she opts for the latter alternative, then she would be as good as dead for me and her mother.

O God, guide my path and dispel the uncertainty which cripples my mind and paralyses my movements.

> *Such is the guidance of God: He guides therewith whom He pleases, but such as God leaves to stray, for him there is no guide.*
>
> Qur'an, s. XXXIX, 23

... MY PRAYER was answered; a word from Mr Saba, received through a messenger this morning, told me that he had comforting news. It could not but be about 'Aisha so I dropped everything I was doing and hurried along to the dragoman's office. That was my first visit to the British Consulate. I was escorted by a *kavass* to Mr Saba's office, where I was met by this naturally congenial man. Knowing my distress, however, he did not lose much time on civilities, and said, 'I have news for you. 'Aisha is well; she and 'Ali are among his people . . . they are in Jabal 'Amil. To be more precise they are in a town called Tibnine, east of Sour (Tyre).

'If the idea occurs to you to go after your daughter in that part of the Provinces, I advise you not to. You would be in mortal danger. Even the Governor's soldiers cannot go there unless welcomed by the local *beys*.

'Forgive me if I am brutally frank, but your safety is more important than anything else now that the harm has been done.'

The moment I heard that 'Aisha was alive – which was all I had wanted to hear until then – my feelings changed; I resented and even hated her. Resentment and hatred are normally directed against a person alive, which explains why those unnatural feelings were kept at bay as long as I was not sure about 'Aisha's fate.

I brushed those terrible thoughts off and looked round for the first time since I entered the room. To my utmost surprise, I realized that I was sitting on a high chair facing Mr Saba, who was himself seated behind an elevated desk, beneath the portrait of his young Queen hanging on the wall. I thought to myself what an uncomfortable and unnatural way to rest, and what a terrible fate that is, to be ruled by a woman; no wonder her country ranks only second after the dominion of our Master, the Sultan of Sultans and the Lord of Two Continents and Two Seas.

Unconnected ideas of this kind often occur when grave events unfold. I did not allow them to take hold of the situation, and immediately reverted to the more serious subject, saying, 'I cannot thank you enough for bringing me news of 'Aisha and for your concern about my safety. Nevertheless, I must go to where you located her and find out whether she is, at this moment, detained against her will, has regretted her madness and is prepared to beg for forgiveness and come back with me. Despite the danger you warn me of, I am still willing to take a chance. Who knows, maybe these wild people will have pity on a grieving father.'

'If you have set your mind on this dangerous expedition, I will not let you go on your own,' said Mr Saba, who reflected a moment and then proceeded: 'I presume you will be going to Sour by boat. Once in that town, you will give a letter from me to the keeper of the *khan* which is located on the seafront. A trustworthy guide will be provided for you and will accompany you to Tibnine. You can rely entirely on the man; he is from the area and I have known him for ages . . . he is the one who, at my request, found out where 'Aisha is.'

I thanked the dragoman and hurried home to make preparations for my dangerous but nevertheless essential journey and to warn my uncle of my impending arrival.

. . . PRECEDED BY my young servant, who was holding a lighted lantern with one hand and a bag of provisions with the other, I made my way to the port. It was just before dawn and the city was still asleep. The streets were deserted, except for a few bony stray dogs scavenging for food among the heaps of refuse which could be found everywhere and were endlessly replenished whenever rain and decay reduced them.

The sailing boat I had hired the day before was waiting to take me through the first leg of my journey, to Sayda, where I will spend the night at my uncle's. From there we will progress to Sour to join the guide provided by Mr Saba; from Sour, God will be our sole protector.

As I boarded the boat and the crew prepared for sailing, a few exploring rays of light sprang from behind the Mountains. After making sure that the terrain would be undisputedly its own, the sun slowly and majestically emerged from its resting place and established absolute dominion in a matter of seconds, blissfully unaware that its conquest would not last for more than a day. Its swift triumph was marked by an explosion of radiance which overawed nature for a brief moment; therewith an orgy of birdsong, corrupted by sporadic and pretentious cocks' crowing, marked the beginning of another day.

In an hour or two the heat would be unbearable and all creatures would long for a little shade. We sailed for Sayda, closely following the coastline. When we arrived within sight of the region of Jiyeh, the tomb of Nabi Yunus (the Prophet Jonah) could be clearly seen from the boat. This Prophet, who was swallowed by a big fish, was safely landed on this sandy beach after having repented and glorified God.

I saw in the remarkable story a good omen for the safe return of 'Aisha. With God's mercy and help, she will also repent and return from darkness to daylight.

> *Had it not been that he (repented and) glorified*
> *God, he would certainly have remained inside the*
> *Fish till the Day of Resurrection.*
> Qur'an, s. XXXVII, 143/4

Finally we landed at our first destination and I was happy to be reunited with my uncle. His health, however, worried me. He did not look to be in good shape, and I presumed that he might not be able to accompany me on the strenuous and dangerous journey ahead. Soon he reassured me by telling me of the arrangements he had made for our trip, and we spent the rest of the day reminiscing about the past and talking about my mother. He never mentioned my father, but the fact that he alluded several times to the fortune he has made in exporting tobacco to Egypt left no doubt in my mind that he intended to vindicate himself, and prove to the son that the father was wrong to spurn him.

I had too many recent worries on my mind to linger over an old family feud, hence I retired into my room.

. . . THE SURFACE of the sea was perfectly calm, so when we entered the bay of Tyre we could see a surprising number of granite columns that lie in the waters. We landed safely and went straight to the *khan* which was yonder, outside the walls of the city.

The innkeeper took the dragoman's letter from me and promised to make the necessary arrangements forthwith. My uncle wanted to see a business acquaintance of his, and invited me to join him. I chose to stay and to try to have some rest. All of a sudden, I felt very down, for I realized the temerity of my enterprise. I was about to put myself at the mercy of people who are detaining my daughter, expecting from them understanding and pity. What a foolish prospect.

The innkeeper interrupted my brooding and outlined for me the route he has devised for me with Hussein, the guide. It goes like this: we will start on our journey tomorrow, immediately following the *salat al-'asr*, when the intensity of the heat will have died down.

'Why can we not leave early in the morning?' I asked.

Our host explained why, in these words: 'We feel you should not go to the *bey* in Tibnine unannounced, for you never know how he will react to your presence. Hence we recommend that you leave tomorrow in the early afternoon and encamp near the village of Kanah for the night. Hussein will proceed to Tibnine, meet the *bey*, explain to him the purpose of your visit and spend the night in the town. The morning after, he will come back to you and brief you about the *bey*'s disposition. Either you go ahead with your planned visit or you return to Tyre, depending on his report and on your gut feeling.'

Reassured by the cautious approach, as outlined by the innkeeper, I decided to take a stroll by the seaside before the sun set. A light breeze blew from the west and alleviated the summer heat. Absorbed in my thoughts, I walked on the edge of the water where the sand is bearably hot. On the one hand, I am utterly convinced that it is my sacred right to ask for the return of my daughter, but on the other, I know by experience that right does not always prevail. I am myself aware of that only too well; there was one particular instance when I denied justice and that continues to haunt me, even though it took place many years ago, when I was a young judge eager to please those who could further my career. It was that poor woman whom I deprived of her daughter's custody with no justification, just because her powerful father-in-law requested that favour from me, and I granted it to him.

Surely the trying situation I am faced with is the punishment that God has sent me for my ill deed. O God, take notice of my contrition and let this difficult moment be my sole punishment, and do not deprive me of my daughter for ever.

> But those who do ill deeds and afterwards repent
> and believe – Lo! for them, afterwards, Allah is
> Forgiving, Merciful.
>
> Qur'an, s. VII, 153

. . . OUR PARTY left Tyre when the sun started its slow descent towards the horizon. My uncle, myself, Hussein, his son and five mules – one for each of us and the fifth one loaded with our provisions and equipment – commenced the ascent of the hills in the direction of the village of Kanah. Soon the plain, the city and the sea stretched out at our feet. What a beautiful panorama it was, and how much more I would have enjoyed it in different circumstances. As one looked at the sloping declivities, ruins and vestiges of civilizations – long risen and long gone before Islam – caught the eye. One of those vestiges is the tomb of the King of Tyre who supplied much of the material intended for building Solomon's Temple.

Close to Kanah we turned to the left and saw some curious sculptures in the face of the cliffs on the south side of the ravine which comes down from the village. They were some twenty figures of men, women and children, carved in the rock. No one was able to tell me whom they represent.

Nearby we established a camp and Hussein departed for Tibnine, leaving us in the capable hands of his son. I am tired and worried, about 'Aisha's safety and about my own. With fear in my heart, I am making this entry in my diary by the flickering light of the fire started by Hussein's son to keep at bay the wolves, panthers and leopards which prowl about this region.

God is my protector and in Him I put my trust.

*Allah is the best Carer and the Most Merciful of
those who show mercy.*

Qur'an, s. XII, 64

... HUSSEIN CAME back to our camp some time after sunrise; he brought with him comforting news. The *bey*'s reaction to our proposed visit was to say that he would be extremely honoured to receive us and to invite us to stay in Tibnine as his guests as long as we wish. My uncle was not entirely reassured; he asked Hussein whether the *bey* could be trusted. Hussein's reply showed signs of his commonsense.

'Usually,' he said, 'the *bey* can be trusted with regard to his invitation, which implies that no harm will befall us. Your daughter's homecoming is a different matter altogether. Although I have told the *bey* about the nature of your visit, he did not make any comment.'

With that we struck camp and took the direction of Tibnine among the oak and terebinth trees. The town came into view after we gained the summit of a long ravine. It appeared crowning an elevated *tell*, and commanding a vast area of the surroundings. The *bey*'s palace dominated all the town's structures. We crossed the dry ditch which ran round the *tell* and entered the palace. Once there we were immediately conducted to the *bey*.

When we were brought to his reception hall, he sprang from his elevated divan and greeted me and my uncle as if he had known us for ages. We responded in kind. The *bey* was an agitated fat man with congenial manners, but on occasion he was unable to hold back from darting chilly eyes at his interlocutor. During such moments his cordiality would become false and therefore frightening. During the exchange of civilities, Hussein and his son stood several steps behind us, showing marks of deep respect and submission. The reception hall was full of people, who made room for my uncle and myself to sit at the right-hand side of the *bey*. At his left sat an elderly cleric who was introduced to us as Sheikh Hasan.

I was dying to tackle the actual reason for my presence there, and to request that 'Aisha be returned to me. Proprieties did not allow me to do just that, so I waited for the right moment to come.

The *bey* himself was not in a hurry to listen to the object of my visit, to say nothing of the fact that our presence had obviously eased the boredom of his daily life. He turned towards me and said, 'Sheikh 'Abdallah, it would be foolish of us not to take advantage of your presence here – a presence which greatly honours us – and more foolish not to try to learn from you as much as we can. We would greatly appreciate that you, an authority among your people, tell us, from what sources do you deduce the law?'

The compliments did not deceive me and the question put me in an uncomfortable position. I replied, 'O grand *bey*, I am neither an *usuli* (theoretician of the law) nor a *kalami* (theologian). I am a simple jurist who relies on the work of eminent predecessors, who in turn have derived the law from the Book, the *Sunna* and *ijma'* (consensus).'

'What if you are unable to find an answer to a given matter in any of those sources, would you then use *ijtihad* (subjective reasoning)?' asked Sheikh Hasan, joining in the conversation.

'Only if, by *ijtihad*, you mean *qiyas* (analogical deduction). A reasoning which relates to a ruling from the Qur'an or the *Sunna* is the only valid *ijtihad*,' I replied.

'What about *'aql* (reason)? Do you not realize that God has created reason as the means of divining the law? Do you not believe that no decision derived through the process of *ijtihad* could be deemed legally valid unless it is found in conformity with *'aql*?' interjected Sheikh Hasan.

I felt myself trapped in a discussion which I could not conduct as freely as I wished. I searched for a way out, and assistance came from my uncle, who said, 'Sheikh Hasan strikes me as being a learned scholar with a knowledge as wide as the sea. My nephew – as he acknowledged himself – is but a simple jurist who is content to follow the opinion of the prestigious predecessors of his school. The debate is unequal; I request its postponement until the time I come back to you with Sheikh al-Ansari from Sayda; he is an *usuli* and he would be a debator worthy of Sheikh Hasan. Only then should we expect a contest befitting an assembly as eminent as this one.'

The *bey* smiled as a sign of acquiescence and I felt it opportune to bring in the topic for which I have made this painful journey, and endured the opprobrium of a real interrogation. I said, 'O noble lord! Account of your justice has spread around all the Provinces. There is no corner of the mighty empire which has not heard of your magnanimity. Would you allow that a father be deprived of the sight of his daughter?'

'What can I do for you? How can a person living in this remote place be of assistance to a distinguished man from the city?' he asked.

The confirmed liar was well aware of the aim of my visit, so his words boded no good. However, I had no choice but to pretend that I believed his offer of assistance was genuine. I related the story of 'Aisha's disappearance from home and, summoning up all the courage I could muster, I said that I had been informed that my daughter was in Tibnine with the man who had abducted her.

The *bey*'s reply resounded: 'In Tibnine I would never permit the marriage of any girl or woman without the permission of her father or guardian. I commiserate with your anguish; I am a father myself. But it is obvious that you have been misled. I can assure you your daughter is not here.'

All the hopes I had nurtured suddenly collapsed. What I had dreaded to hear, but had put to the back of my mind, was made plain to me. I will never see 'Aisha again. No pain, no anger, no frustration could be more intense than what I felt at that moment. Yet I could not vent my feelings. I could not tell my villainous host what I really thought of his vehement protestations of honour and rectitude. All I was able to say was, 'There is no power and no strength except in Almighty God.'

The *bey* invited us to stay as his guests as long as we wished, but warned us not to leave the palace unaccompanied, because – as he put it – his people were not accustomed to seeing strangers and were dangerously suspicious about any questioning. I expressed the desire to leave immediately. Hussein, however, objected that the sun was already low on the horizon and a journey in the darkness in this wild country, and in the present circumstances, could be extremely hazardous. Not willing to face the prospect of spending the evening in the dreadful company of the *bey*, I pretended not to be well and retired with my retinue to one big room arranged for us, with the understanding that we would leave early in the morning.

Dinner was served, but Hussein dismissed the servants and did not allow us to eat anything of what they brought. That night he lay down across the room's door in such a way that an intruder would have to step on or over him and wake him up in the process. My guess is that if he ever slept, it was with one eye open, so worried was he for our safety.

At dawn we hurriedly left the palace, and were about to pass the houses located at the outer limit of the town, when I saw in the embrasure of a door a form, all wrapped in white, who looked in our direction and then slowly turned her back and vanished in the inner darkness of the house.

'That is 'Aisha,' my heart told me. 'That is her,' I said aloud. My uncle pressed his mule against mine, urging the possibility of only one direction – that is, forward. Hussein guessed more than understood the meaning of my shout, so he hurried on the party without waiting for further explanation. Soon we lost sight of the town. It was a broken man who reached Sour and asked to be left alone to weep in peace, and pour his despair and sorrow into his diary.

Ramadan 1259 (September 1843)

Return to Beirut; violation of a British house;
murder of a go-between; campaign of slander against
the Qadi; Abu Kasim to the rescue; a visit to
As'ad Pasha . . .

. . . I AM VERY GRATEFUL to my uncle, for despite his poor health, not only did he accompany me on my distressing journey in search of 'Aisha – a journey which ended in failure and disappointment – but, in addition, he has insisted on escorting me back home. What I dreaded was to face Umm Khalid on my own, for besides everything else, I was unable to tell her where 'Aisha was and, wherever she might be, whether she was there under constraint or there of her own volition. The prospect of confronting Umm Khalid was only part of my torment; several questions kept creeping into my mind with no answer for them: Did I give 'Aisha all the attention a growing girl needs? Had I totally lacked insight and sensitivity when I failed to realize that 'Aisha's chronic illness was not in her body? Did my abrupt announcement of her imminent marriage to Abu Kasim precipitate her insane deed? Only Allah knows.

My concern about Umm Khalid was to prove unfounded, for it was an Umm Khalid totally submissive and resigned who met us at the door of the house. Soon I was made aware of the reason for her unexpected state of mind; for two consecutive nights she had dreamed the same disturbing dream. She saw 'Aisha wearing the dress she had chosen for the wedding ceremony, surrounded by several women in white. Then 'Aisha's image faded away and the women in white started weeping and lamenting loudly while beating their chests, in the same way that hired mourners act at funerals. Umm Khalid sought elucidation of that recurring vision from an elderly woman renowned for her skill in the science of interpreting dreams. What she heard was the ominous advice not to expect 'Aisha's return, ever.

Hence the disappointing news I brought with me came as no surprise to Umm Khalid. Her attitude induced me to reflect more intensely on my plight. It was the beginning of the month of Ramadan, the blessed month during which the Qur'an was sent 'as a guide to mankind', a time for the spiritual discipline of fasting, when God's grace is closer and more easily accessible to the true believers. Unworthy of that grace as I was, I had to purify my heart, submit to His will and follow the path determined by Him. Guidance and solace I had to seek from my *Sufi* master; without him I would be like a blindman among a herd of wild animals, or like an ass which untiringly turns round the well, draws from its water but cannot quench its thirst.

Sheikh 'Abdel Rahman, fully aware of my predicament, greeted me with God's words and a slight reproach in his voice.

> '*Truly it is in the remembrance of God that hearts find reassurance.'*
>
> Qur'an, XIII, 28

I made repentance for having questioned Allah's designs and, urged by my master, meditated the verse of the Qur'an he had quoted and repeated with him the Divine Name till reaching the state of ecstasy.

Having found peace of mind, I realized that Umm Khalid's vision was a sign from God telling me that 'Aisha, the faithful daughter I once had, no longer existed, and that I should cease all quest and adjuration for her return.

During the evening prayer I submitted myself to the Will of God, repeating His own words:

> *'But ye shall not will expect as God wills . . .'*
> Qur'an, s. LXXXI, 29

. . . MY QUIET RESIGNATION and that of Umm Khalid brought peace to our hearts and alleviated our shame, but did not dispel our profound sadness.

The next step that my uncle and I took was to visit Abu Kasim in order to render an account of our unsuccessful trip to Tibnine. We went to his place some time after the sun had set, to give him enough time to absorb a meal after a long hot day of fasting. He already had a visitor, in the person of Abu Ibrahim. The atmosphere in the room was congenial and I surmised that both men had settled the financial matters which opposed Abu Ibrahim's nephew to his divorced wife, Abu Kasim's sister. I felt rather unhappy, for if something of that sort had taken place it was without my intervention; at the same time, I knew that an arrangement was to be expected, for Abu Kasim would never accept that his social standing should receive blow after blow without a swift reaction. With the shame brought to him by his financée's disappearance, he could not afford to remain on bad terms with the powerful Abu Ibrahim. Soon the latter confirmed my guess and, by the same token, aired his antipathy for me when he bade me the following welcome: 'Abu Khalid is willing to work towards the amicable settlement of any sort of dispute except for the one which is close to home.'

I was taken by surprise by this abusive attack, but Abu Kasim did not give me time to reply. He said, 'I am sure that Abu Khalid is the first to rejoice about our family reconciliation. If he did not partake in the meetings which, with God's help, ended up with our complete understanding, it is because he has had so much on his mind recently.'

Abu Kasim's words should have had the effect of appeasing

my anger. In fact, what they did was to create another worry for me. Abu Kasim's unconcerned tone when he spoke about the disappearance of my daughter, his bride-to-be, made me realize how much his reactions would always surprise me, even after a relationship of more than forty years. I should have known that Abu Kasim was not the sort of man who would assume the consequences of an adverse situation, and that at the first opportunity he would distance himself from the annoying problem, without looking back and without any guilty feeling about those left behind.

After Abu Ibrahim left the gathering, Abu Kasim did not ask me about 'Aisha and I felt more dignified in saying nothing in view of his apparent lack of interest.

When we ourselves departed, my uncle looked at me and said, 'By God, in all my life I have not seen a more selfish man. What a cool customer indeed!'

... ABU IBRAHIM'S intolerant faction is in the ascendant. More often than not, there are incidents which illustrate the narrow-mindedness of the masses, manipulated by a handful of merchants and silk-loom owners who complain that foreign trade competes with them unfairly. I do not agree with their view, for competition brings down the prices of goods and that benefits the multitude of customers. It must be for that reason that our enlightened Sultan decreed that European goods would incur a favourable customs' tariff. Most certainly what he had in mind was the good of the greater number of people, compared to that of a handful of individuals. Of course, no sensible policy as such could be welcomed by those who see their profits diminish.

The whole atmosphere in town is unhealthy and it has even affected the troops. Anti-European feeling is running high. Yesterday some ten soldiers stormed the house of Mr Nash, the well-respected British merchant. They were after his Arabic teacher, who, they alleged, insulted them.

Some of the soldiers guarded the door, others took

possession of the courtyard while their leader, with a subaltern, proceeded to the room where Mr Nash and the teacher were sitting together. They seized the latter, whom they beat violently, despite Mr Nash's strong protests, and endeavoured to drag him away from the column which he held. At that moment a servant girl made her appearance and struck the two men with her wooden clog. Painful blows showered on the two assailants, who turned away from their victim and against the servant. The teacher had time to effect his escape from the roof of the house into the street.

Thereafter Mr Nash persuaded the soldiers to withdraw and went straight to Colonel Rose to complain. The British Consul addressed a note to the Governor, who summoned the *majlis* for tomorrow.

... THE PASHA seemed extremely annoyed about the incident which took place in Mr Nash's house. In fact, all the *majlis*'s members shared the same feeling. Colonel Rose had requested the imprisonment of the two assailants, coupled with the degrading of the officer and the summary punishment of the subaltern, for they have assaulted a person who enjoys the temporary protection of the British Consulate because he was attached to the household of an English gentleman.

In addition, the British Consul wanted from the Pasha the severest injunction to the troops and police that they should respect the Europeans in general, and even refuse to arrest any of them or their dependants at the solicitations of the natives. Instead, any native with a claim of whatever nature against a European, or a person protected by a European, should apply direct to the civil authorities.

As expected, Abu Ibrahim stood against punishing the two soldiers and against any injunction of the kind requested by Colonel Rose. The Pasha asked the view of all the *majlis*'s members and, when it came to me, I stood with the Consul's requests, which I believed to be well founded and justified.

Eventually it was that view which prevailed and earned me

Abu Ibrahim's vindictive look, which made me shiver. That man has become a sworn enemy, and he does not even have the social decency to hide his animosity. Henceforth I shall have to watch my step and, most of all, I shall have to be more careful about my relationship with the dragoman. Never mind if it means that I will see less of Mrs Saba in the flesh, so long as she can be a part of my fantasies.

... THE WHOLE TOWN has only one topic of conversation, the slaying of Mariam the Jewess. When after a full day she failed to appear outside the rooms where she lived, and from where she worked, her neighbours forced their way into her place and found her lying on the floor in a pool of blood. Her throat was cut and terror, which must have struck her at the moment of her death, was encapsulated in her open, glassy eyes. She must have been dead for several hours, for big black flies were buzzing around her dead body, summoned by the intense heat and attracted by the smell of blood and the creeping process of decomposition.

... MY UNCLE left us for Sayda this morning. At daybreak I accompanied him to the port and strongly clasped him to my heart. I had the sad feeling that the few days we have recently spent together could well be the last instance of such encounters.

He is the person I turned to for help during the most difficult time of my life. He was immediately available and placed himself at my disposal. Maybe I took unfair advantage of his kindness and asked too much of him; the trip to Tibnine, and then to Beirut, might have irretrievably damaged his health. In a sense I am glad to have renewed bonds with him, but at the same time I fear that this revival might render the ultimate separation more cruel and more difficult to bear.

My worries were probably exaggerated, for when he boarded the boat he was relaxed and good-humoured, as if a heavy load had been taken off his tired shoulders. His final words left me puzzled, because I could not understand their full meaning, and I did not have time to ask him for an explanation. These were his exact words: ''Abdallah, my son, every human being passes through crises during his lifetime. Either he sheepishly submits to adverse circumstances or he courageously tries to bend them to his advantage. I can see that you have chosen the latter approach.'

... I AM VERY APPREHENSIVE, for I believe I have discovered the meaning of my uncle's farewell speech. I sensed that people I came into contact with were ill at ease in my presence, and that conducted conversations – most likely about Mariam's murder, for there is no other topic nowadays – ceased the moment I entered a room. Then I realized, in a flash of intuition and to my great horror, that her murder was, if not directly imputed to me, at least linked to her role in 'Aisha's unsanctified love affair.

This diary is not intended to be seen by any human eye, thus when I started it I vowed to be unreservedly candid about what would be in it. I say, before God, that I had nothing to do with the dressmaker's death. I am innocent of her blood. To pretend that I deplore her ill fate would be a lie. However, I refuse to assume responsibility for an event which occurred by God's will. I took no part whatsoever in it, but it has to some extent soothed my grief.

Above all, I refuse to assume any responsibility on the account of a gypsy girl's ravings; my fateful encounter with that diabolic creature and her reading the palm of my hand must have been images of a bad dream, or, if they ever took place, the result of a dreadful curse. There is no other explanation for her pointing a finger at me before any blood was shed. Unsanctified thoughts on their own cannot be detected, let alone penalized. If it were otherwise, every human being would infringe the law at one time or another.

I am aware that it is not enough to protest my innocence in written words not intended for public notice; the truth must

127

come out, and will come out with God's help. Is it not He who said:

> *Nay, we hurl the Truth against falsehood, and it*
> *does break its head, and behold falsehood does*
> *perish?*
>
> Qur'an, s. XXI, 19

. . . I DO NOT KNOW to whom to turn for the sympathy and assistance which I will continue to need until the truth manifests itself with God's help. The only person who has my actual confidence is Gerios Antoun, whom I fully trust with my money, but who can never be the recipient of my intimate secrets and the witness of my worries.

That leaves Abu Kasim as the only other person I can turn to in this trying hour. Certainly I was hurt by the apparent lack of interest he displayed after 'Aisha's disappearance, but what else could be expected from a man who is extremely sensitive about the image he projects to others? The more unconcerned he pretends to be about an unpleasant or unfavourable event, the less his image will be tarnished. That is at least what he believes, and he conducts his life accordingly. He should know better; he should have realized by now that his protection from malicious gossip, vexing jokes or more serious harm is not his demeanour and the appearance he puts on, but his wealth and standing in society. Without them he would have been as vulnerable as any other man.

I regretted not having gone to Abu Kasim sooner; his welcome was as friendly as usual and he declared his readiness to rouse for my sake all the support he could muster. He had heard rumours and gossip connecting 'Aisha's disappearance with Mariam's murder, but he almost completely reassured me by saying that anyone who knew me would never hold, even for a moment, that I could have anything to do with a violent death. Laughing, Abu Kasim added, 'My friend, you are not reputed for your physical courage; besides, everyone knows how cautious you are. You lawyers do not take risks; you are bad businessmen, bad lovers and certainly not of the pugnacious species.'

For the first time in days I smiled and felt comforted. 'What do you advise me to do to dispel the nasty rumours which are spread against me?' I asked.

He replied, 'What I will do is to accompany you on a visit to the Pasha. Once there we will stay as long as practically possible; then we will leave the *diwan* (reception room) with large smiles on our faces. News of our lengthy visit will spread like fire and everyone will know how high you stand in the Pasha's esteem.

'No such step could be a success without a proper gift; thus, as a prelude to our visit, I will send to As'ad Pasha, in your name, a pair of precious Persian carpets, which I have recently bought in Damascus. The carpets are expensive ones but that will be the only way to bring a smile to the Pasha's face.'

I kissed Abu Kasim, vouching to repay him for his kindness and generosity.

Bless you, Abu Kasim, my friend, bless your clear judgment, good sense and down-to-earth way of confronting difficulties.

. . . AFTER SUNSET we went to see As'ad Pasha and found his *diwan* full of courtiers and solicitors. Even more numerous were the parasites, those people who hang around a person in power – no matter who that person is – lest they languish away from the often false sense of security provided by association with the mighty ones.

The Governor's reception was more courteous towards me than usual and warm-hearted towards Abu Kasim, as was customary. He made a most considerate gesture, for he took me and Abu Kasim apart, to a smaller adjoining room, where we were served refreshment, coffee and sweets, and offered pipes.

The Governor very civilly thanked me for my gift, whose worth seemed to have been properly assessed. For more than an hour he talked about trifling events in the Province and he was, as usual, extremely well informed; with his usual skill, Abu Kasim kept the conversation going on in that direction for as long as he could. I was delighted with all that time spent in the Pasha's company, for the longer he kept us, the higher I was likely to be elevated in the esteem of my fellow citizens and my name kept at a distance from any unpleasant subject.

Eventually the Pasha turned to more serious matters and said, directing his words to me, 'Sheikh Abu Khalid, I heard that you have turned down a litigant who came to you with the expectation that you would resolve a dispute which opposed him to the monks of a monastery located in the Christian district, about the cost of water supplied for the irrigation of his field. He wanted justice from the *sharia* court and you denied it to him, sending him back to judges he does not trust because, he believed that with them, his adversaries can easily tip the balance of justice in their own favour.

'You have to understand that the *sharia* court has ordinary jurisdiction. Whenever a litigant from the Mountains expresses the wish to be tried before that court, his preferences should be respected. These are my instructions, and they will stand until Christians and Druzes settle their differences about the jurisdiction in the two districts.

'I expect you in future faithfully to comply with those instructions and not to listen to Zaid or 'Amr.'

These last words made me apprehensive. Could they mean that the Pasha was aware of the conversation I had with Mr Saba when I visited him at home, and when he suggested that I should send back to their natural judges any litigants from the Mountains? I remember well, no one else was there, because Abu 'Abbas arrived later. The Pasha's last words must have been a figure of speech, and did not imply that he had any particular information about the matter. Obviously he had been informed of the judgment I had rendered with regard to the case of the unpaid use of water, and he was telling me what to do concerning subsequent cases. Why on earth should I always try to give any particular event an interpretation other than the obvious one?

The best attitude I could think of was to indicate to the Governor that I had understood his words not as a reprimand for the past, but as tracing a line of conduct for the future. So I said, 'Your wisdom has no measure, and your decision is the wisest possible. I will scrupulously follow your directives, which will lead to the triumph of the *sharia*.'

The Governor smiled and accompanied us to the door, amidst sidelong glances of envy from those around.

... THE END OF RAMADAN brought the usual joy and festivities, coupled with a string of family and social visits. Festive time is the perfect occasion for anyone who is someone to test his standing in society. Part of the test is to ascertain who visits whom. Important people are visited and seldom leave their homes during a time of celebration. Another part of the test for those who expect to be visited is to receive the greatest possible number of well-wishers. It is said that some notables even hire known touts, who herd people to them by spreading the news of some recent favour bestowed on those notables. But often a prosaic bait, such as the promise of coffee and sweets lavishly offered, is enough to attract a crowd.

I stayed at home, anxiously awaiting the test's result. The turn-out was rather disappointing. Far fewer coffees and lemonades were served this year compared to last. My visit to As'ad Pasha might have toned down ill-disposed gossip, but it did not bring me back into popular favour. I do not know the reason. It could well be that a hostile party is working against me and poisoning the whole town's atmosphere by taking advantage of one unfortunate event after the other.

Does such a party really exist, or is it a figment of my imagination? And if it exists, who could be behind it? Abu Ibrahim is the most likely candidate to assume that nefarious role. No one except God knows for certain, because *God has knowledge of all things* (Qur'an, s. IV, 176).

The one person who has never failed to pay me a formal visit during Ramadan, from the time he came to live in Beirut, is Abu 'Abbas. He honours me with his respect during Ramadan and I scrupulously repay him in kind during *'Id al-Adha* ('the feast of the sacrifice').

His visit this year will probably be the last, for he told me that very soon he will be going back to his village in the Mountains with his entire family. He was not sure that his decision was timely or even wise, for the political situation in the Mountains is far from being stabilized. Practically speaking though, he does not have any other choice, for not only does he have vast properties there to look after but the Yazbaki clan to whom he belongs needs his presence and his advice, the situation being extremely volatile between the Druze clans, on the one hand, and between the Druzes and the Maronites on the other.

Abu 'Abbas was ill at ease. That demure man who normally hides his inner thoughts was showing slight signs of anxiety. I was sure that the reason was not personal to him but arose from fear for peace in the Mountains. I will sincerely regret losing the company of that honest man and I wonder if I will ever see him again.

One person I did not see was Mr Saba. He had sent me a pile of sweets as a gift, together with his apologies for not being able to present me personally with his best wishes for the occasion.

Shawwal 1259 (October 1843)

*Reward offered for catching the dressmaker's assassin;
illegal exercise of judicial functions; riot in town; Abu
Ibrahim's accusations; the Pasha is deeply dissatisfied;
the dragoman makes himself unavailable . . .*

. . . A PLACE to see people, and be seen by them, and to sense
where one stands in the social scale and in the favour of the
mighty ones, is the public *hammam* of Bab al-Serail. Once there
I passed through a succession of rooms where heat gradually
increased. The first room had the same temperature as
outdoors, the second one was slightly hotter, the third one yet
more sultry, until I reached the last room, where the steam of
boiling waters exuded from marbled basins and filled the
sweltering air.

I was bathed by two attendants, then my body was covered
with a large white piece of cloth and I was taken to the rest
room to relax and cool off before leaving the *hammam*.

It was there I expected to see and hear the reaction of the
regulars, to listen to their conversations, examine their faces,
often not being able to meet their shifty eyes, and eventually
realize exactly where I stand in public opinion.

I saw the *Mufti* lying down on cushions in one corner of the
room; next to him was one of his confidants. Both men got up
in slow motion, looking at their feet, and left the place,
hugging the wall. That message was well received. I sat next
to a man who I thought would be as considerate as usual; he
was that, and much more than necessary, and his exaggerated
attention and forced joviality made me ill at ease. I longed to

run away from these specimens of contemptible meanness and base opportunism, but I forced myself to stay a little longer, otherwise my departure would amount to a shameful retreat.

I moved aside and sat, my back against the wall, beneath a small opening which communicated with the adjacent room. I closed my eyes, for I had seen enough – not realizing that I could still hear words which would make me perceive things even more sharply than with open eyes. With my eyes shut, my sense of hearing became more acute and I was able to hear a conversation conducted in the connecting room. After a few exchanges, I recognized the two speakers by their voices and from the few hints dropped during their discussion. They were Abu Mazen, Abu Kasim's cousin, and Bakr Kronfol, the man who had complained to me about his neighbour's facility to overlook his premises, and in whose favour I had adjudicated.

Kronfol said, 'I was told by the Chief of Police, who heard it from the Governor himself, that the medical man who was sent to Jerusalem by the British philanthropist (Sir Moses Montefiore) has put up a reward for anyone who will lead to Mariam's assassin . . . You know, they are all Jews.'

Abu Mazen exclaimed, 'What a remarkable sign of solidarity! Could you ever imagine that the fate of a poor dressmaker would raise the interest of a great man living in a faraway country? I wish we had someone similar here . . . Hundreds, thousands of human beings die, sometimes in atrocious conditions, and no one, whether in office or not, shows any sign of pity or interest.'

'Hush, hush, what kind of words are those . . . do you want us to end up in gaol, or worse?' interjected Kronfol, who then proceeded: 'You do not understand what the reward means; as usual you ride the high horse of justice. What I am interested in is to discover who killed the Jewess; big names may be involved and, who knows, you may soon be appointed Qadi yourself, and be given the opportunity to put into practice your sense of justice. Ha, ha, ha!'

I was dumbfounded by Kronfol's onslaught. Here was a man

to whom I had just done a valuable good turn and he was anticipating my downfall with jubilation. I wondered how Abu Mazen, whom I hardly know, was going to react to that! To my utmost surprise, Abu Mazen's words were most dignified and soothing. This is what he said: 'I do hope that the murderer will be caught; I do particularly hope that I do not know him. Until we are told for sure who committed that criminal act, I would refrain from making hasty accusations.'

Kronfol did not concede defeat. He vehemently objected: 'Do you think that I do not have proof of what I said? I am not that childish. I was told by Abu Ibrahim stories about your friend which will make you reconsider your judgment, or, I had better say, will make you have a positive one instead of being all the time on the sidelines.'

Abu Mazen was obviously unimpressed, for he replied, 'He is not my friend but an acquaintance. Once or twice I have seen him at the house of Abu Kasim, who praises him very highly; that I know. I know also that Abu Ibrahim has a grudge against him and that his stories have nothing to do with the dressmaker's murder. Please, let us talk about something else. We are here to relax and not to hold an open court about an event whose circumstances are yet to be fully disclosed.'

Al-hamdu lil-illah (God be praised), there remain in the world people like Abu Mazen, who abide by His words:

> *God does command you . . . when you judge between mankind that you judge justly.*
>
> Qur'an, s. IV, 58

. . . MY COURT'S CLERK arrived at the *mahkamet* (courtroom) in a great state. The news he brought was extremely upsetting. He told me that he had just heard that an *effendi* (a title of respect usually given to a learned man) had set up a law court, close to the al-Dabbagha Mosque, the Mosque of the Tannery, in one of the poorest and dirtiest parts of the city, and conferred upon himself the title of Qadi. I have heard that man being called a demagogue, with little or no knowledge of the law, and I had no doubt in my mind that, if the information was correct, the incident would be another of Abu Ibrahim's dirty tricks. I quickly cleared my workload for the day and sent the clerk to ascertain through his eyes what he had heard with his ears.

An hour later he came back in an even greater state. He was out of breath and, when able to speak, he told me that he saw a large crowd all over the place around the mosque. When he got closer he saw the *effendi*, cross-legged on a carpet spread out in the open air. He was protected from the heat by the shadow of one of the mosque's walls, and distributed justice amidst cheers and shouts of defiance.

I asked what kind of slogans he had heard. He seemed embarrassed and avoided answering my question, which I had to repeat. I was then told that the mob was expressing satisfaction at having a judge who could understand their needs and protect them from foreign competition and baleful influence; at the same time, the crowd pledged to challenge, by force if necessary, any attempt to compel them to forsake the Qadi they had chosen for themselves.

The matter was very serious and frightened me. My first reaction was to think that I had to do something, but after reflection I decided to go home instead and stay there, leaving the resolution of the crisis to the Pasha.

I hurried to my family and, for the first time since 'Aisha's disappearance, I asked Khalid, Umm Khalid and Khadijah to stay with me while I was having dinner. The moment I convinced myself that the illegal exercise of judicial functions was not my problem but that of the authorities, I felt much relieved. However, I needed the comfort which emanates from people who will remain on your side whatever you do.

The Pasha has no other option except to re-establish order, otherwise he would be at the mob's mercy with regard to any other incident. Knowing the Pasha, he will never allow such a state of affairs.

Greatly heartened, I enjoyed the stew and the rice prepared by Umm Khalid; and while I was eating, I hugged Khadijah several times, for I needed the warmth of loving contact, as much as she needed it herself.

. . . As EXPECTED, the Pasha sent troops to arrest the impostor and disperse the crowd. But it all went wrong; the mob round the masquerading Qadi formed a dense circle which the soldiers were unable to penetrate or dissipate. Skirmishes followed, but the mob stood firm and even attacked the soldiers, who retreated. The impostor's followers were elated. They spread out of their sector and went on a rampage in the street where money-changers and money-lenders have their booths.

When the looting ended, and while the rioters were on their way back to their area, unfortunate chance so ordained it that they encountered the funeral procession of a *dhimmi*. The deceased was carried by the mourners and not on the back of a donkey, as had been required previously before the custom was abolished by the Egyptians. The mob went berserk and attacked the procession, leaving two dead and many wounded among the mourners. They finally retired to what they believed to be their safe haven.

That was too much for the Pasha and the Consuls to bear. Troops cordoned off the rioters' sector, and the *majlis* was summoned to meet forthwith.

I was full of apprehension as I sat among the members of the *majlis*. I knew that some of my colleagues would take advantage of the shameful situation and put the blame on me. I endeavoured not to show my anxiety and sat poised and collected, waiting for the assault.

Naturally, it was Abu Ibrahim, always lying in wait for me, who led the attack. He reproached me for my leniency with regard to matters in which the *sharia* had left no room for subjective appraisal and quoted, as examples, the cases of Yehya, the apostate who later repented, and of Zahra, who was given back to her Christian natural parents. He also criticized me for what he described as a subservient attitude towards people who have foreign interests at heart. He did not name those people, but he was obviously and mainly referring to my friendship with Mr Saba. Abu Ibrahim stopped short of mentioning 'Aisha's disappearance from home directly, but he ended his diatribe with the following words, which hurt me most: 'When a person is unable to rule at home, he cannot be a judge among people. The people have sensed these flaws and have elected their own Qadi. They are ready to fight to keep the choice they have made.

'We have to look at this matter from the angle of public order and the welfare of the community. The situation demands that Abu Khalid resigns and devotes his time to the studies he is so fond of.'

I wanted to reply and defend myself, but As'ad Pasha did not give me the opportunity; he adjourned the meeting and dismissed us with these words: 'My first priority is to quell the civil disorder, which is, fortunately, limited to a small part of the town. I ask all the members present here to contribute to re-establishing order – and I know that they can do that – otherwise they will have to bear liability for what might happen when force is used, and it will be used if necessary.

'We cannot request Abu Khalid to resign under the mob's pressure, or under any sort of pressure. Once everyone has returned to his home, including the *effendi*, we will discuss what to do next with the office of Qadi.

'Believe me, no suggestion will be taken into account unless it has Abu Khalid's approval and blessing.'

I was not deceived by the Pasha's polished words, which only gave the appearance of being in my support and in favour of my rescue. Beneath the veneer the meaning was visible. The Governor does not want my resignation under public pressure, but he will welcome it once that pressure is lifted.

My fate is sealed, short of a miraculous intervention.

The first thing I did when I returned home was to send

word to the dragoman, telling him that I urgently needed to see him.

. . . IT WAS ABU KASIM who called on me and informed me of the Pasha's real disposition. I was right in assessing the true meaning of the Governor's closing speech; what he really wants is for me to leave office quietly in a week or two.

I discussed with Abu Kasim possible ways of reversing this distressing situation and making the Pasha change his mind. Each way led down a disappointing blind alley. Nevertheless, I did not resign myself to accept defeat, and declared that I would go to Mr Saba and request from him that he urge Colonel Rose to use his influence with the Governor in my favour.

Abu Kasim looked at me with commiseration and said, 'Do you really believe that they would do that for your sake? My dear 'Abdallah, for them we are but lemons that are thrown away, once they have squeezed and drained the last drop of our juice. Do not count on any help from that quarter.'

Pride and bravado made me say what must have appeared to Abu Kasim as utterly ridiculous, in view of the circumstances: 'You have no idea,' I said, 'how strong are the ties of my friendship with the dragoman. He owes me a number of favours and I am sure he will be only too happy to pay his debt.'

Abu Kasim looked at me with yet more commiseration and said, 'Whenever confronted with a problem, you have always examined its less favourable aspects and expected the worst to happen. Your experience as a lawyer makes you proceed that way. The cases brought to your court are, most of the time, instances of relationships which have turned sour. Nobody comes to you to tell you any good news about his business or his family. I mean by that that you are no stranger to the negative aspects of matters in general. The problem you are facing now is definitely a difficult one and requires objective scrutiny. I am not asking you to be a pessimist but a realist. Let us analyse together all possible angles, especially the negative ones. Let us assume your Mr Saba is not willing to help, what do you intend to do?'

My reply was more childish bragging: 'I will not resign and people will rise in my favour and eventually justice shall prevail.'

Abu Kasim was definitely not impressed. He continued more firmly: 'You will do nothing of the sort. You will leave your office with dignity. I promise you, you will not stay idle for long. In our world favour and disfavour, good days and bad days alternate as surely as darkness follows light. No one stays in one state for ever . . . social death, political demise, shame and disgrace, as well as their opposites, are all transient conditions. I know that you have a modest fortune; that will allow you to wait comfortably for better days. Your fortune will protect you against the harshness of the bad times to come. Make good use of it, be generous, "give food to the mouth and the eye will shy away".

'I want your promise that you will contact no one, but will do what I have told you to do.'

. . . DESPITE THE PROMISE I made to Abu Kasim I have sent another word to Mr Saba, urging him to fix an appointment for us to meet. The reply came that the dragoman is extremely busy for the time being, but will contact me when he has the time.

. . . WHEN SEVERAL DAYS had passed without any news of the dragoman, I mustered all my courage, swallowed my dignity and headed for his house. It was late in the afternoon when, by his normal habit, Mr Saba would have awakened from his siesta and would be sitting in his garden or living room, depending on the weather, surrounded by attentive visitors. More than once I was about to abandon the idea of my unannounced visit and retrace my steps back home, but an involuntary impulse made me proceed and reach his door.

I was told by the black slave who opened the low-lying door

and introduced me to the closed courtyard that Mr Saba was out of town. Unexpectedly, I felt relieved, and was about to turn my back and leave, but the servant interrupted my move with these words: 'My mistress is here if you wish to see her.'

I was stunned and delighted at the same time. Never have I been invited to meet a lady unrelated to me and, what is more, in the absence of the master of the house. I remained silent for a while, not knowing whether I should take advantage of this amazing invitation.

The servant got impatient and exclaimed, 'I am going to bring my mistress,' and then left without waiting for any reply. Before I could get hold of myself, Mrs Saba appeared in the courtyard and, with her customary grace and conviviality, invited me inside the house.

I was utterly embarrassed and did not know what to say, or even where to look. My hostess tried to put me at ease and inquired about Umm Khalid's health and the children in general, which was a way to avoid mentioning 'Aisha's name. She was too urbane to ask about the aim of my visit, but also too clever to let a courtesy call drag on for ever, so after a while she put an end to the polite greetings with these words: 'My uncle's son (my husband) went to the Chouf Mountains, where he will be staying for several days. He is completely overwhelmed with work owing to the delicate situation which prevails in the Mountains. He is so dreadfully worried about the possibility of a renewal of clashes between the inhabitants of those Mountains that he has had a row with the Pasha himself about the latter's policy. Now he cannot ask from him even the smallest favour.'

I believed her words were a deliberate message, thus I tried to regain my composure, and whispered, 'I am here to see if I could be of any assistance during these worrying times. Please tell Mr Saba that if he needs me he knows where to find me.'

I was angry with myself because of the absurdity of my offer. I, who could use any help, from whatever quarter, had foolishly extended a ridiculous offer of service to a man whose assistance I had come to beg. The only consolation I had was that I might have saved face by reversing the objective of my visit – which now appeared senseless after the veiled message I had received.

When Mrs Saba offered me a glass of lemonade, all of a sudden Abu Kasim's words – that we are, for the likes of the dragoman, but lemons which are thrown away once used – rushed into my head. I declined the drink and left in a hurry, knowing that I would never see Mrs Saba again. Amazingly, this thought did not affect me one way or the other. The predicament I have lately experienced has made me more aware of the true nature of mankind and killed not only my illusions but also my dreams.

POSTSCRIPT

Abu Khalid's diary came to an abrupt end at this point. We know, from later chronicles, official documents and private papers, that he resigned the office of Qadi under pressure, but that he was subsequently brought back several times from obscurity to be entrusted with high office. At other times he suffered disfavour, and was once even condemned to exile, which, however, did not last long.

He lived on into old age and made a large fortune from the various positions he held and through the good offices and advice of Gerios Antoun. He took as a second wife Abu Kasim's divorced sister, who bore him three sons and two daughters.

The most likely reason Abu Khalid did not keep his diary beyond October 1843 is that after that date, and following a period of profound bitterness, he devoted his time to business and no longer saw the relevance of scrutinizing his inner self or examining others' behaviour. His doubts and irresolution had gone, but also his touching humanity. He wrote no more.

A contemporary, anonymous Jewish chronicle tells us that Mariam's murderer was never caught and that, after a while, nobody cared.

Glossary

asadi: silver *asadi* piastres minted during the reign of an Eygptian Sultan, Mamluk. They were called *asadi* because one of the two faces bears the image of a lion (*asad*).

bab: lit. gate. In the context of this book it designates one of Beirut's gates. The city had seven gates which were partially destroyed and became obsolete when, from the mid-nineteenth century onward, the walls and fortifications were knocked down either as a result of acts of war or to make room for more buildings.

bey: honorific title, basically given to a governor or administrator of a Turkish town, province or district.

Capitulations: concessions granted by the Ottoman Sultan to Europeans who lived in Turkey's dependencies, and to subjects of the Sultan who benefited from European protection, allowing them to enjoy extraterritorial rights and favourable commercial treatment.

Deir al-Kamar: a town in the Chouf Mountains, which in the nineteenth century was populated mainly by Christians.

dhimmi: a non-Muslim belonging to the category of people

living in the Islamic state and under its protection. The two largest categories of *dhimmi* in the Ottoman Empire were the Christians and the Jews. They were granted autonomy of institutions and protection under Islam, subject to certain restrictions and the payment of specific taxes.

diyya: compensation, or blood money, paid by or on behalf of one who has committed homicide or wounded another.

dragoman: part of the diplomatic corps with specific missions to act as interpreter and to provide knowledge of local customs and habits. He was often a local Christian. *Dragomans* were also recruited among nationals of the foreign consulates with a knowledge of the Turkish and Arabic languages.

faqih: a specialist in *fiqh* (see below).

fiqh: the science of Islamic law; jurisprudence.

Franks: name given by Orientals to all Europeans.

hatti-i shariff of Gulhane: decree issued in 1839 by the Sultan 'Abd al-Majid (1839–61), promising basic civil liberties and an equitable system of taxation to all the Empire's subjects, whatever their religion or sect.

ijma': consensus of opinion.

ijtihad: the use of (subjective) reasoning.

majlis: council.

manzul: a quarter separate from the main lodging and intended for visitors and guests. Only close family and close relatives, such as brothers and uncles, were admitted to the main lodging of a Muslim family in the nineteenth century.

Mountain or *Mountains* or *Mount Lebanon*: These all designate the chain of mountains which, from the north to the south of modern Lebanon, runs parallel to its Mediterranean shore.

mufti: a person learned in the *sharia* who provides an answer (*fatwa*) to a legal or theological question. He was held in high esteem and could be consulted by anyone, whether a litigant or not. There were instances where even the Qadi consulted him. The *fatwa* must have an absolutely objective character and not address a particular case.

qiyas: analogy: analogical deduction.

riba: usury.

salat: the ritual prayer, accompanied by a series of movements, repeated several times. *Salat* is to be performed five times daily. *Salat al-fajr* is the dawn prayer and *salat al-'asr*, the afternoon prayer.

shehada: the statement of belief in the dogma of Islam.

shuhud al-hal: witnesses (usually more than two and less than ten) who have as their sole function the task of remembering the details of the proceedings, besides the clerk of the court, who draws up concise minutes of each case.

Sublime Porte: the term commonly used in the nineteenth century to designate the whole of Ottoman government. It referred more particularly to the building which in the middle of the century housed the offices of the Grand Vizier, the ministries of Foreign Affairs and the Interior, and the Supreme Council of the Judicial Ordinances and its successor councils.

Sunna: Deeds, utterances and tacit approvals of the Prophet Muhammad.

tazkiya: the inquiry made by the judge about the moral standing of witnesses called upon to testify in court. Testimony was accepted or rejected by the judge according to the result of the inquiry he had undertaken.

'uqqal (sing. *'aqil*): Druzes are divided into *'uqqal*, those who know the intricacies of their religion, and *juhhal* (sing. *jahil*), those who do not know these intricacies.

'usma: care and control.

Yazbakis: In Mount Lebanon during the eighteenth century the old rivalry between Qaysis and Yamanis was replaced by the struggle between Yazbakis and Janbalatis.

zawiya: small mosque, school or prayer room.